The Shadow of the Crescent Moon

FATIMA BHUTTO

PENGUIN BOOKS

PENGUIN BOOKS

Published by the Penguin Group
Penguin Books Ltd, 80 Strand, London WC2R ORL, England
Penguin Group (USA) Inc., 375 Hudson Street, New York, New York 10014, USA
Penguin Group (Canada), 90 Eglinton Avenue East, Suite 700, Toronto, Ontario, Canada M4P 2Y3
(a division of Pearson Penguin Canada Inc.)
Penguin Ireland, 25 St Stephen's Green, Dublin 2, Ireland
(a division of Penguin Books Ltd)
Penguin Group (Australia), 707 Collins Street, Melbourne, Victoria 3008, Australia
(a division of Pearson Australia Group Pty Ltd)
Penguin Books India Pvt Ltd, 11 Community Centre,
Panchsheel Park, New Delhi – 110 017, India
Penguin Group (NZ), 67 Apollo Drive, Rosedale, Auckland 0632, New Zealand
(a division of Pearson New Zealand Ltd)
Penguin Books (South Africa) (Pty) Ltd, Block D, Rosebank Office Park,
181 Jan Smuts Avenue, Parktown North, Gauteng 2193, South Africa

Penguin Books Ltd, Registered Offices: 80 Strand, London WC2R ORL, England

www.penguin.com

First published by Viking 2013
Published in Penguin Books 2014
001

Copyright © Fatima Bhutto, 2013
All rights reserved

The moral right of the author has been asserted

The author's retelling of the story of the Greedy King was inspired by reading *Pashtun Tales: From the
Pakistan–Afghan Frontier* by Aisha Ahmad and Roger Boase, Saqi Books, 2008.
Translations of Pashtun poetry were hard to come by and I scoured the Internet for versions and variants.
A lot of the translators and enthusiasts came from blogs, message boards and forums and I am grateful to
all those who shared their love of the Pashto language and its poetry.
The version of the Nazim Hikmet poem used in the epigraph comes from
http://www.youtube.com/watch?v=dyltI3_p4FU

Typeset by Palimpsest Book Production Limited, Falkirk, Stirlingshire
Printed in Great Britain by Clays Ltd, St Ives plc

Except in the United States of America, this book is sold subject
to the condition that it shall not, by way of trade or otherwise, be lent,
re-sold, hired out, or otherwise circulated without the publisher's
prior consent in any form of binding or cover other than that in
which it is published and without a similar condition including this
condition being imposed on the subsequent purchaser

ISBN: 978-0-241-96562-7

www.greenpenguin.co.uk

MIX
Paper from
responsible sources
FSC   FSC™ C018179
www.fsc.org

Penguin Books is committed to a sustainable
future for our business, our readers and our planet.
This book is made from Forest Stewardship
Council™ certified paper.

For Baba
with all my love

For Baba
my soul

My country
I don't have any caps left made back home
Nor any shoes that trod your roads
I've worn out your last shirt quite long ago
It was of Sile cloth
Now you only remain in the whiteness of my hair
Intact in my heart
Now you only remain in the whiteness of my hair
In the lines of my forehead
My country.

Nazim Hikmet

Prologue

In a white house on Sher Hakimullah road eight thirty on Friday morning has come too early.

The bazaar is opening slowly, rearranging its schedule to accommodate Eid's last-minute shoppers. Light drizzle hits the dusty footpaths, carefully, so as not to disturb the shopkeepers pulling up their shutters. The clouds dip low over Mir Ali and, from a distance, the fog makes it seem as though the tanks aren't there at all. On the roofs of the town's buildings, snipers lie in their nests, surrounded by sandbags, their military rain ponchos cold and clammy against their necks, and wait for the day to begin.

Three brothers live under the same roof – a home they share with their widowed mother, who occupies a solitary room on the ground floor, spending her days in the company of a young maid who gives her medicine and homeopathic tonics and twists her long white hair into a single plait every morning.

Two of the brothers are the other occupants of the ground-floor rooms, alongside the family kitchen and a small sitting room. Upstairs, the third brother and his family find their home in disarray as mobile phones beep in lieu of alarm clocks and showers with aged, corroded pipes drip water onto the heads of those who did not remember to fill a bucket the night before. A small cricket bat leans against a bedroom wall, next to a set of plastic cars.

Soggy towels and wet bath mats lie around the bathroom. Socks that stepped in soapy puddles and have to be discarded are strewn on the floor. Muddy footprints of dirty shoes that stomp through the wet-tiled bathroom leave traces of black rings from room to room.

Fridays are always chaotic in the house on Sher Hakimullah road and this morning difficult decisions have been made. The brothers cannot – will not – it is finally decided after some days of deliberation, pray together on Eid.

In Mir Ali, where religion crept into the town's rocky terrain like the wild flowers that grew quietly where no grass ought to have grown, you chose your mosque carefully. Fridays were no longer about the supplicants; they were about the message delivered to them by faithful translators of the world's clearest religion. In Mir Ali nowadays you were spoilt for choice.

There were the mellow congregations, whose mullahs invoked harmony and goodness amongst mankind. These were the mosques that did not keep their flock for long, only enough time to remind them of their duties as a promised people. The sermons might proffer some elementary guidance in such endeavours, but it was largely a drive-through service.

There were the *jumma namaz* mosques that specialized in distinctive foreign-policy-based diatribes – lashings of rhetoric against great satans and the little men who did their bidding. These mosques yearned for converts to their cause but they lost them in Mir Ali, where people preferred to go to the houses of God that had taught their fathers and grandfathers about justice. There was no greater cause in Mir Ali than justice.

One by one the brothers filter into the kitchen to drink their morning tea. White onions sizzle in a frying pan, sweating from the heat. The brothers arrive to claim their place at the small table, draped with a sticky plastic tablecloth, where the day's first meal will be served – sweet parathas and omelettes with diced tomatoes, onions and green chillies. The air smells of the pepper being shaken onto the chopped onions, pungent but sweet. The three brothers take their tea without too much sugar but the aged cook, who brews the tea leaves in a blackened saucepan with fresh goat's milk, ignores them and heaps in palmfuls of refined white sugar anyway.

On the occasion of the first day of Eid, the brothers at the morning table speak to each other in a toneless, secretive mumble. Heads bent low, they don't talk as they normally do, with voices that come with secret smiles and banter that falls out of the mouth playfully. This morning there are few teases and no arguments, only the question of how to proceed with the day ahead.

It is too dangerous, too risky, to place all the family together in one mosque that could easily be hit. They no longer know by whom.

'By drugged-up Saudi pubescents trained in the exact extermination of Shias,' ventures Aman Erum, the eldest brother.

'No, it's not just Saudis,' protests Sikandar, the middle of the three, as he looks around the kitchen for his wife. 'Sometimes there's politics behind it, not God.' She is nowhere to be seen. He swallows his sugary tea uncomfortably.

'Yes, yes, sometimes they're pubescents from Afghanistan. Still Sunnis, though,' jokes Aman Erum, folding a paratha into his mouth as he stands up to leave.

'Where are you going?' Sikandar shouts at him. 'We're eating – come back.' He notices, as he speaks, that Hayat, the youngest brother, hasn't lifted his eyes from the blue-and-green-checked pattern of the plastic tablecloth.

He has to go to work, Aman Erum says, to check in before Friday prayers shut the city down for the afternoon. He reminds Sikandar to pass on his business card, newly printed and designed, to a colleague at the hospital.

'Kha, kha,' Sikandar says, tucking the crisp white and red import/export rectangle into his wallet.

'Wait, which mosque?' Aman Erum asks, turning round and displaying his mouth, stuffed full of the flaky, buttered bread.

'You're going to Hussain Kamal street *jumat*,' replies Hayat, looking up. Sikandar looks at his younger brother's eyes; they are bloodshot. Hayat has decided where each of them will offer his supplications today. He has barely spoken all morning; this is the first time he has broken his silence. 'You know that,' he says to Aman Erum abruptly.

Aman Erum doesn't look at Hayat. 'Yes, yes,' he mumbles, turning away from his brother. 'I know.' The paratha is chewed and swallowed, a hand raised in farewell, and for a second there is a lull in the siblings' chatter as they adjust to the prospect of praying alone, without each other, for the first time.

And then the noise picks up again, seamlessly. The remaining two brothers rise to greet their aged mother, Zainab, who looks around the kitchen as she sits down at the table. 'Where is Mina?' she asks Sikandar as the brothers shuffle around each other to make space for two more cups of chai before their separate journeys through Mir Ali begin.

09:00

I

Aman Erum sits in the back of a battered yellow Mehran taxi and asks the driver to take him to Pir Roshan road. The elderly driver turns in his seat, its brown fabric ripped along the back, exposing dirty yellow foam. 'That's not the address you gave on the phone,' he says, hoping to renegotiate the fare.

There's a spring digging into Aman Erum's back. He adjusts his body against the broken seat. 'Let's get moving, *kahkah*.'

The taxi's windows are all open, but Aman Erum smells something that bothers him. He can't tell what it is. He looks at the greasy side mirrors, held together with strips of duct tape. It's not the slackened seat belts. Aman Erum tries to roll his window further down, but it's stuck. They drive past walls covered in red and black graffiti, political slogans written in thick cursive script. Boys in packs of four and five wrapped scarves round their faces to shield against winter nights as they painted what patches of Mir Ali were not guarded by the military. *Azadi*, they scrawled: freedom.

It has been months since Aman Erum returned home to Mir Ali after a long time abroad. He never thought he would come back.

Aman Erum's childhood in Mir Ali, as compared to that of his brothers, had been idyllic. As the eldest son he had accompanied Inayat to the mosque to meet with friends and relatives every Friday after closing the family-owned carpet shop for the day. And, every summer, Aman Erum had been the fifth member of his father's annual fishing trip to Chitral.

He would lie awake at night throughout the late winter and

7

early spring months, the idea of the trip keeping him company and supplanting sleep. His father and his three friends, men who had grown up within walking distance of each other and whose families were now connected by marriage and children, had been going to Chitral for as long as Aman Erum could remember. He had been a small boy when his father first took him along. Their relationship had been so uncomplicated then.

Aman Erum would load up a light-blue pick-up truck with gas cylinders, tarpaulin from which a large tent would be erected for the fishermen, butter, rice, pots and pans, lentils and vegetables wrapped in sheer pink-plastic bags – enough supplies to carry the men through a five-day camp.

He lived for those summer days. Dipping his feet into the cold river in Chitral, watching his snot turn charcoal-black as he breathed in the fumes from the gas lamps and smoky fires – he never wanted to go home. He remembered blowing his mysteriously coloured mucus into thin tissues and playing cards late into the night.

When he was eleven years old, the summer of an especially bountiful fishing trip, Aman Erum fell in love.

She was twelve and he had never seen anyone so beautiful. Samarra.

He hadn't noticed her until the moment she ran in front of him and hurled her arm upwards into the air, sending the cricket ball in her palm crashing into the wicket and forcing Aman Erum out of a game he didn't even know Samarra was playing in.

Samarra wore jeans and played cricket and rode horses and shot pellet guns and did everything and anything she had seen her father do. When Ghazan Afridi brought home a 150cc motorcycle from his auto shop, saying little of its provenance, only that it was Chinese-made and smuggled via Kabul, Samarra learned how to drive it, relegating her father to the back seat while she tore through traffic, turning corners with the slightest swing of her hips. When Ghazan Afridi went fishing for brown trout in the icy streams of the northern valleys, Samarra held the spotted fish with two fingers hooked into its mouth as it thrashed against the rocks, its gills bursting with fresh air. Samarra never complained; she fought hard and she idolized her father. When Ghazan Afridi brought home Russian assault rifles with wooden hand guards and pistol grips, Samarra sat on the floor, her long legs covered with still unplucked downy hair tucked underneath her, and quietly field-stripped them with her father.

For five days, at the foot of the Hindu Kush's highest peak, Samarra Afridi would be all Aman Erum's. They would sneak out of their fathers' tents at midnight to follow foreigners – tall, sunburned young men with sandy-coloured matted hair hidden under newly bought Chitrali pakol hats – around the local bazaar, which smelled of charcoal, until late into the night. One night as they walked along the Kunar river, Aman Erum slipped, unable to see the path ahead under the ashen moonlight, and cut his hand on the rocks by the bank. Samarra took his hand in hers and squeezed out the blood, the bad blood that would infect his body if not bled out. She dipped Aman Erum's palm into the rushing river to ice it and to stop the bleeding. Before the sun rose, before they had to sneak back to their fathers' tents, Aman Erum and Samarra crawled along the mossy trails on their hands and knees, digging up earthworms for the fishermen's morning excursions.

Ghazan Afridi took the men out on walks and came back with rabbits and small birds they would skin and grill for dinner. He tried to teach Samarra how to cook, but she didn't take to it. Ghazan Afridi couldn't cook either, but never let that get in his way.

When they went back to Mir Ali, abandoning smoky summer bonfires made of cracked twigs and lit with Samarra's cheap plastic lighter, Aman Erum imagined he would lose Samarra to her pack of neighbourhood friends and devoted followers. He had seen the children on their bicycles circling round her home straight from school, still wearing their uniforms. But Samarra left them to their bikes and Aman Erum watched from the window as she walked towards his house.

Samarra never once looked back at the children on the bicycles who called her name, shouting for her to stay with them. She walked straight across the gravel with her head held high, craning her neck to see if it was Aman Erum she spied at the window. When Samarra saw him she smiled, but didn't wave hello. Instead, she walked faster, kicking the pebbles out of her way with every step. Aman Erum could still hear her friends calling out her name.

Samarra stood at his door, her palms pressed against the knitted metal of the screen door, and waited to be invited in. Aman Erum put down his books.

'Salam.'

He didn't know quite what to say. Samarra was his first visitor.

As dusk drew over the shade of the pine trees and Ghazan Afridi called across the street for his daughter to leave her friends and come inside, he found only a gaggle of schoolchildren. None with his daughter's messy hair or spindly arms.

The taxi lurches over speed bumps hastily constructed in the middle of already rutted, unfinished roads. The driver opens the glove compartment and takes out a dirty cloth to wipe the rain off the steering wheel. Aman Erum touches the torn fabric of the back seat. He recognizes the smell. The taxi reeks of petrol. Aman Erum doesn't want to dirty his *shalwar kameez*, freshly laundered and starched. He doesn't want the cloying, acrid smell hanging off him today. The drizzle falls in through the cracked window, wetting Aman Erum's face. The broken spring digs into his back again.

Aman Erum never made it into the bicycle gang; he was awkward and uncomfortable around other children. Instead, he wrote Samarra poetry, small verses in her geography copybook in school – a class he now shared with her as he had been promoted a grade above his year – and declared himself lost in love with the twelve-year-old girl whose hair was always messily tied in plaits. Aman Erum lived for the summers when Ghazan Afridi would bring his daughter to Chitral.

But Ghazan Afridi began to take longer trips out of Mir Ali. Samarra had been her father's constant companion, his lodestar, but he left her at home more and more now. Samarra was too old, too much of a woman to accompany him. It was dangerous, he said. Samarra wasn't afraid. She wanted to go with her father anyway. But Ghazan Afridi left Samarra with her mother, Malalai, taking his Chinese-made motorcycle on odysseys he never spoke of afterwards.

'Wait,' he said, pinching the air with his fingers. 'The coming years will bring Pakistan to its knees.' Ghazan Afridi told Samarra to be patient. They were building something big. He drove the motorbike up to Jalalabad one summer, journeying alongside the Kunar, leaving Samarra alone at camp.

Aman Erum didn't have to wait for Samarra to come to him then. There was no interminable hanging around and killing time, sitting, as he had become used to doing, in front of the honeycomb screen door in Mir Ali, listening for the sound of her footsteps on the pebbles outside his house, with books piled on his lap, the weight of them deadening his legs.

'What if we lived here?' Aman Erum asked one midnight outside their fathers' tents. 'What if we just stayed?' For as long as he could remember he had felt constrained in Mir Ali. He wanted to get out, to be free, to make money, to move without checkpoints and military police poking their red berets into your car and asking for your papers. The other boys of Aman Erum's age didn't seem to feel confined by the country's wild borders; they didn't feel restricted the way he did.

Samarra laughed. Even in the dark, Aman Erum could see the spotty pink of her gums. 'This isn't our home.'

'But we could make it our home. I could be a guide, set up a business. Take travellers through the passes.'

Aman Erum knew about the mountains, he knew how to navigate the forests. Inayat had taught him how to magnetize a needle, rubbing it on wool cut from the sleeve of a sweater for three minutes until his fingers went numb. Inayat would watch as Aman Erum laid the needle on a leaf, making a compass to guide them through the unknown wilderness. His father had taught him maps of the land, drawn from memory and measured in footsteps, not miles. Belonging. Inayat thought his son would find belonging in this cartography of the heart. But Inayat was thinking of a different boy, a much younger son.

Aman Erum was fifteen. He had been dreaming up escape plans since taking his first trip out of Mir Ali many summers before. Chitral was all he knew of Pakistan so far. But he had seen a magazine photo spread on Bahawalpur, its sandstone palaces lit up with fairy lights, its magnificent forts and blue and white shrines. He had read about the port in Karachi, about the ships that sailed there from Greece and Turkey full of cargo, and the highways that connected the green plains of the Punjab. He would go anywhere. He didn't care where, but he didn't want to spend his life in Mir Ali.

'You can't do that.'

Samarra was sixteen.

Aman Erum stared at her green eyes, unlined except by her thick lashes. A dark-brown speck of colour escaped her iris. Even this, Aman Erum thought, looking at Samarra under Chitral's pale moonlight, was beautiful. Her spindly arms had filled out and her voice had grown up too. Samarra pronounced her words slowly, almost languidly. Aman Erum turned away from her and looked out over the valley.

'Of course I can. I've been coming here since I was a boy. I know the terrain and the trails. I've been hiking with Baba since – I don't know. Ten years? There are so many travellers out here on their own. How do you think they're getting around now? No one's taking them to the best spots, where there're carp and rainbow trout and the open –'

Samarra, whose hair was no longer in plaits but now loose round her shoulders, interrupted him.

'No, you can't choose your home. You can't just make a new one.'

Aman Erum was quiet. She didn't understand about the future.

Samarra, who no longer wore jeans, stood up and cleaned the grass from her *shalwar*, wet in patches from the dew. 'We have a home.'

Her words were swallowed by the night. Aman Erum wasn't listening.

The summer Samarra turned seventeen, she didn't come to camp. No one had seen Ghazan Afridi since the spring. He had packed his motorcycle with enough food for a week's drive. He waved goodbye to his wife as she stood at the doorstep and kissed his daughter's hand. Think of me, Ghazan Afridi said. He touched her hand to his eyes. Ghazan Afridi didn't say where he was going; he rarely did those days. Think of me. That was all he said. It was all Samarra ever did.

The fathers considered delaying the trip, breaking the tradition to keep vigil for Ghazan Afridi, but in the end they went. Who knew when he would return? Who knew if he would? And in what shape?

'It might be months. It could be years, even,' Aman Erum said to Samarra Afridi by way of commiseration as he packed for the trip.

Rolling the tarpaulin neatly onto the back of Inayat's light-blue pick-up truck, Aman Erum said the word *years*. Samarra had heard people gossip; she had heard them say that Ghazan Afridi had another family across the border. She had heard people say he had other children. That he had been running training camps. Taking money from other countries, from other states. She had heard all those things, and she'd been happy to hear them. Nothing was worse than what she imagined.

'Maybe years, Samarra – most probably just a few months, but even if it's years, he'll return.'

He loaded the truck and nodded his head. 'Maybe years.'

But Ghazan Afridi never did come back.

Aman Erum climbed into the back of the truck, and sat holding a jerrycan of petrol between his knees. He envied Ghazan Afridi. He had got out. It almost didn't matter to Aman Erum how. He was so sick of Mir Ali. 'Samarra, you know more than any of us that he'll return.' He spoke to her as he adjusted the can, pointing the nozzle away from him and making sure he had enough space to stretch out his legs, but when he looked up he saw Samarra had already left. He couldn't see her but he heard her footsteps fading on the pebbles outside his house.

Aman Erum wrote Samarra poetry until their adulthood brought their communication by letter, and therefore unchaperoned, to the notice of the grown-ups who guarded their children's hearts.

Samarra never wrote a single line of poetry back to her

beloved. She allowed Aman Erum's serenades and consented to receive every stanza and story as a necessary diversion, but she was too heartbroken to reply in verse. Samarra would not go to university like Aman Erum. She would stop at matric, a tenth-grade education which the world had decided was more than enough for a seventeen-year-old beauty who would never, they hoped, have cause for further studies. Her life would be blessed, they imagined, and she would not have the time to study once married and living in her husband's home. Perhaps Ghazan Afridi would have returned to see his daughter settled by then. Wouldn't she like that? Wouldn't that be nice?

Samarra wouldn't complain. She would study on her own, at home, reading second-hand physics books bought at the small bookstall at the bazaar that sold comic books and dog-eared copies of Rahman Baba's poetry, and doing exercises in used exam workbooks until eventually the elders had no choice but to relent and allow her to attend the local university, provided she stopped after a Bachelor's degree.

Aman Erum had applied, quietly, to the army. It was a secret attempt to flee. He was young, he had no record, his mother's family was clean. He thought they might take him out of Mir Ali and into one of their cadet colleges. Two things happened. First, he was turned down. The army didn't want men from these parts; they didn't even have a recruitment office in Mir Ali then. The officer Aman Erum had spoken to, the lone man in khaki green on duty at the base, had laughed in his face.

So, first, Aman Erum had been turned down, and second, Inayat had found out. Aman Erum never knew how his father discovered his attempt to enlist in the armed forces – he hadn't said a word to his mother or brothers – but Inayat knew. Discussing his second option, his only viable option, at the kitchen table one evening Aman Erum spoke of studying commerce at the local university.

'It would be a step, obviously. I'm not going to study commerce just so I can stay in Mir Ali and haggle over the price of carpets. It would give me the foundation to apply for further studies abroad. Yes, fine, it will be expensive but if I work hard here perhaps I can get a scholarship.'

Aman Erum devoted more time to thinking about himself as he grew older and became bolder about expressing his desires. Sikandar, the middle brother, had been listening and holding a broken-off bite of *rotay* in mid-air.

'How much do you think?'

Aman Erum considered the question. 'I'd have to pay – it would be lakhs – even with a scholarship, but probably only the cost of housing and living.'

At that, Inayat, who ate very little, only some yoghurt with his *rotay*, pushed his plate away. 'You will have to pay for your choices, Aman Erum, much more than you realize.'

The words hung between them.

Aman Erum's heart started to beat fast, too fast. He looked at his own plate, filled with food he hadn't touched because he'd been so busy talking. He picked up a piece of lamb, a small charred *boti*, and put it in his mouth.

Inayat placed his hands on the table and lifted himself out of his chair. He left the kitchen without another word.

The only way out for Aman Erum, then, was business. He had to earn his way out. Aman Erum was the eldest son, the one who would set the way for his brothers to follow, a way out of the carpet business the family had struggled in for decades – and which was now endangered because of the halting of trade routes and the army's insistence on being given a share in the transportation of rugs across the Northern Frontiers.

'*Askari* Carpets!' laughed Aman Erum's father, his hair a bright white from the roots of his scalp to the down of his beard and neatly trimmed moustache. 'Imagine that,' he said, and laughed less confidently, more softly.

'They will have put their fingers everywhere, even on the ground on which we stand and the fibres through which we weave our stories.'

Inayat had fought in the first battle for Mir Ali in the 1950s, and had survived. He had fought amongst the bravest, against the nervous young soldiers of Pakistan's new army. He had raised his young sons on the stories of Mir Ali's struggles.

'After a fortnight of camping in the hills and peaks on our bellies, ducking bullets and trading fire with monstrous machines, we would dust off our shawls that doubled as elbow rests and mufflers and pillows and welcome in the next regiment that came from the city to take our place. After donating our leftover tea leaves and warmest winter protection, we walked an hour and a half to the doorsteps of our mothers' homes.'

'Did you go back?' Aman Erum must have been fifteen. He was only a boy.

For many years after that conversation, Inayat shook with the memory of this question, a query Aman Erum did not even remember making.

'Did we go back? Did we go back?'

Inayat shook his head and ran his hands through his hair.

Aman Erum did not remember asking if the rebels returned to the battlefield. But later in life, as he began to withdraw from Mir Ali, he remembered other questions from his teenage years.

'The next two decades we spent in hiding, in torture camps, in unknown and unmarked cells across the country.' As his body aged, as his shoulders drooped and the white hair of his eyebrows grew, and as Inayat's lungs strained against his ribcage, he committed the remainder of his life to passing on the memories of a youth lived in battle, fighting for Mir Ali.

'The state did not wait, this time, for a rebel band to cross a frontier and plant a flag or issue a proclamation of independence and self-rule. This time they came to us first. They waited for the lull in fighting to settle in fully. For us fighters to take off our magazine clips, our rugged boots and camouflage and return to the daily lives and uniforms that took us to work as professors and shopkeepers and economics students and plumbers. And then they sent the soldiers in.'

Thousands of them, in convoys of armoured vehicles, weighed down with garlands of assault weapons and hand grenades, flooded into Mir Ali. They came in conquering battalions and in plain clothes. Aman Erum knew the story by heart.

Doors were broken down in the dead of night, men were kidnapped from their streets, women were widowed and children were orphaned to teach the town its most important lesson: there was no match for the ruthlessness of the state. Another generation of male warriors would not grow in Mir Ali.

Inayat brought himself to tears as he spoke.

'Some of the elders were able to escape across the border to Afghanistan; some of their sons joined them and were eventually hunted down – killed and left to bleed on faraway soil and buried in no-man's-land. For a time, till the late seventies, the state believed – truly believed! – that they had beaten the rebellion out of the people of Mir Ali.'

'Haven't they?'

Aman Erum remembered this question now.

'Haven't they already?'

And he would never forget the silence that followed.

Inayat did not tell Aman Erum his stories from then on. Inayat was a sentinel of Mir Ali's history; he checked for those with whom his nostalgia might be shared and for those to whom it should be denied.

'Don't isolate the boy,' Zainab begged her husband as she watched him take their youngest into his memory, nightly feeding Hayat the stories while Aman Erum was left to his schoolbooks. 'You're excluding him.'

'He's too angry,' Inayat would say quietly. 'He counts my defeats.'

'Aman Erum is just a boy,' Zainab argued. 'He won't understand why you speak to Hayat about these stories and not to him.'

'He understands.'

Inayat would shake his head and say quietly, 'He understands very well, Zainab.'

Mir Ali's history continued like this.

Most Pakistanis thought of Mir Ali with the same hostility they reserved for India or Bangladesh; insiders – traitors – who fought their way out of the body and somehow made it on their own without the glory of the crescent moon and star shining overhead.

But the shadow of that moon never faded over Mir Ali. It hung over its sky night after night, condemning the town to life under its cold shadow.

Mir Ali had stalled. Aman Erum refused to be stymied alongside it.

Aman Erum wanted to leave. He wanted a stamped passport out of his strangled home. But he said, convincingly, that it was only the opportunity to work freely that he wanted – a living that could not be threatened away.

He could make a business anywhere, he told his mother, who knew nothing about free markets but often dreamed of the world. He could take a flight to Australia and set up an international travel agency marketing itself towards immigrants, those whose home countries did not feature on routes advertised at Qantas office desks or listed on their computers.

He could go to Canada – there were immigrants there too, living in empty, undecorated homes – and import local handicrafts that would be a reminder of the landscapes left thousands of miles away as they built their new Canadian lives.

England. He had heard of neighbours' sons who left for England and worked in corner stores and restaurants until they built neighbourhoods out of their enterprise. It would be easy, Aman Erum told his family, his young brothers, once he learned the international language of business.

His brothers, younger by months and then by years, followed his plans avidly. Sikandar even silently marked Aman Erum's university textbooks as his own for when he also earned a place to study commerce. Together, he and Hayat waited for invitations to be offered, for chances to become partners in Aman Erum's yet-to-be-named, yet-to-be-established international businesses.

But Aman Erum's invitations never came without a price.

'The Pir Roshan road *jumat*?' the taxi driver says, turning his head so the passenger, who has not stirred in his seat or moved his eyes away from the window, can hear him. 'It's not what it used to be. The sermons are short and uninspired. Why don't you go to the Sulaiman mosque instead? I can drive you there. The imam is very spirited, fiery, much better.'

'One of my brothers is going there. I'm going to Hussain Kamal *jumat*,' Aman Erum says, as he follows Mir Ali's roads intently. He doesn't look at the taxi driver, a jaundiced-looking fellow with a brown woollen sweater over his wrinkled *kameez*.

'So why not go with him? What are you doing going to that

far-off mosque when you could be with family at Sulaiman *jumat*?'

'Too dangerous.'

He turns his head away from the window, just a degree, to meet the frown of the taxi driver's eyebrows, a look almost permanently stitched to the man's forehead.

'In case something happens.'

Aman Erum clears his throat. The sentence is stuck in his windpipe and needs to be ejected properly. Does he sound paranoid?

No one goes to the vegetable market with their mother; she goes alone and carries the thin plastic bags of over-ripened aubergines and salty karela on her own, her arthritic knuckles turning white with the weight of the vegetables.

No one works at the mechanic stall their father built with his sons' hands, after the death of the family's old carpet business, a death that came after Aman Erum's refusal to take it over – as he is often reminded. They take shifts when things pile up for their father's old manager, who still runs the shop. But no longer do Aman Erum or his brothers stand together over burned engines, smoking cigarettes through fingers stained with toxic grease and sweat.

No one prays together, travels in pairs, or eats out in groups. It is how they live now, alone.

The taxi driver's forehead falls; his eyes understand.

'I don't go for Friday *munz* any more. It's better not to. Allah will exempt us. He has already exempted us. He has exempted and misplaced and forgotten everything that came to Him from Mir Ali, from the frontiers of this country within a country.'

Aman Erum doesn't want to get into it.

But the taxi driver has already started. 'The state lies while promising autonomy – more than autonomy! – and decentralization so that each province can regulate its own affairs. And now he's coming here today, that crook of a minister is coming *here* and using words like "democracy", "reconciliation", "devolution". Does he think we are simple people, that we will think those words are promises? Does he think we won't notice that they have come up with a new way of using our own people against us?'

Aman Erum doesn't want to talk about the visit. It's all anyone has been interested in talking about for weeks now.

'*Khair*,' the taxi driver continues, 'at least the media tries not to treat the people of Mir Ali like total barbarians. They at least speak of us with curiosity. That, and pity for our uninspired youth.'

'What else can we do?' Aman Erum shrugs.

'There are some who know.' The taxi driver's eyes look at his passenger in the rear-view mirror. 'Know what to do and how to do it. Believe me, *zwe*, we have legions of them.'

'What next? What now for Mir Ali?'

Inayat had refused to answer his eldest son.

'Don't tell me you think there's a way out of this? That you can keep going?'

Inayat had always known what would happen next. They all knew, those men who lived out their youth in mud bunkers drinking murky rainwater and tea leaves, what would come of their struggle.

The state would begin to fight its own.

Town by town, civil wars were lit by the wide-scale violence of the army – a violence that spanned decades and finally reached its zenith in the War on Terror. Swat, Bajaur, Deer, Bannu . . . one by one they all rose up against the state.

'The army didn't even see it coming,' Inayat said as he leaned his body across the kitchen table, taking Hayat's hand in his own. 'They cannot see how they created this. How they gave life to our insurgency.' Inayat pressed his son's hand.

Mir Ali, when its moment came, rose to right a historic wrong. The district and the town that was its heart would rally. Mir Ali would fight. 'Everything we in Mir Ali know about our lives will have to change,' Inayat said, preparing Hayat for the struggle ahead. 'We will teach our children to live with curfews and midnight raids, prepare the elderly for moves at three in the morning, abandoning our homes and possessions. Each and every member of the household will know that pain is of no consequence when fighting for the collective.'

Hayat was ready. Hayat had always known it was his destiny above that of all the others. His eldest brother cared for nothing else besides his studies, his business opportunities, his faraway options for livelihood – selling dirt-cheap knick-knacks from his hometown at inflated prices or fleecing visiting tourists when the mountain climate was right and the river was swollen with rainbow trout. He was of Mir Ali but had decided very early on never to make his future here, only his fortune.

Though they all sat with their father at the kitchen table long into the evening, as the old man spoke to them in parables, it was Hayat who understood the meaning of the words and listened beyond the cadence of his father's voice while the electric heater trembled beside them.

Inayat never spoke to Hayat of the future, he spoke to him of the past, of the obscene projections it had made upon the present and he knew his son, who grew taller and taller and whose hair grew longer and longer if Zainab did not insist upon a visit to the barber, did not need to be inspired.

Hayat did not speak of Mir Ali, he listened for her.

He listened and watched for others who, like him, were waiting to be brought underground so that they could be enlisted to protect her. But when the call came, it came from home. Mir Ali will not be abandoned by her sons, Inayat told Hayat as he gave the movement his own.

Hayat had already heard in school that men settled far from home, working as kitchen staff and *sokidars* across the country, sent their wages without being asked. Shias who had left, feeling threatened by the Sunni movements that had sprung up around the Northern Frontiers, sent their sons back to Mir Ali. 'All in the service of brotherhood,' he told his father. Hayat felt close to the moment. The battle for Mir Ali was no longer restricted to panegyrics at Inayat's knee.

Sikandar, meanwhile, had given up his borrowed dreams of business for medical school. He studied night and day to pass his board exams. He wanted to make something of himself; he wanted to be a part of something too. But he wanted it to be regulated, secure. Business – Aman Erum's idea of business at least – was too risky. It dabbled too much in the unknown for Sikandar's liking. There was no need to travel far from home. Sikandar saw plenty of opportunity here. He was at the top of his class at medical school. There simply wasn't time, he explained to Hayat, for him to get involved just now.

But Hayat wasn't looking for company. He only wanted news of the rising rebellion. As the months passed and the fighting intensified, he heard that those who lived abroad, making better lives for themselves, had returned home to fight. Women, men and children, there were no timid souls to be found amongst the hopeful of Mir Ali. Their time, as the generations who had struggled and suffered saw it, had finally come. But not all welcomed the honour to fight, to die, for Mir Ali.

Samarra never travelled out of Mir Ali any more. There were no more summers in Chitral, no more motorcycle drives along the Kunar, no more presents brought from Kohat or Peshawar and wrapped in old newspapers lingering with the scent of Ghazan

Afridi's winter leather jacket. In the early years of her father's absence, Samarra dutifully restricted her life to home. She spent her late teenage years tending to her mother, Malalai, and trying to convince her of the things she knew to be true. Uncles – distant cousins and family elders – came with handouts every so often, rupees tied with rubber bands or stapled so that the notes, imprinted with the unsmiling visage of Mohammad Ali Jinnah and soggy with *paan* stains, tore. It is our duty, they said solemnly. A few thousand every month, enough to pay the bills, to keep Samarra in school. But even when the money petered out, even after Samarra's mother began to teach and cook and sew to supplement their thinning finances, relatives came several times a week, accompanied by neighbours or old associates of Ghazan Afridi. They came to show their faces to Ghazan Afridi's forsaken family and to condole with them.

At first, Samarra helped her mother receive the visitors politely, bringing them tea upon a tray and tissues to wipe their unnecessary tears. Malalai never failed to cry when receiving her husband's cousins and their wives.

'Don't cry,' Samarra whispered to her mother as they stood at the door once the guests had left. 'Don't cry,' she whispered. 'Nothing ever happens to the brave.'

But Samarra could not control her mother's tears or hem in her mourning. She could not convince her that nobody knew anything, that there was no body, that Ghazan Afridi could only be alive. You don't cry for a man in hiding. You don't mourn for a man you have not buried.

Samarra could not stop the visitors from bringing food and comfort every week. So she did the only thing she could. She stopped serving the tea. She stayed in her room and counted time.

Samarra never stopped waiting for Ghazan Afridi to return.

By the time Samarra was twenty-one, it seemed that every-one was fighting to leave Mir Ali. She tried to share in Aman Erum's excitement when the news spread in Mir Ali that he would be travelling to Islamabad to receive a study visa for America. She told her girlfriends that he would make a new life for himself and that it was what he always wanted. And when he came back she would marry him and they would settle in Mir Ali as a family. Things are changing, she said to the girls, who were already wearing engagement rings on their fingers. She believed it too.

She knew it was the answer to the question of what their lives would be. It is the only way, she told her girlfriends, that Aman Erum will be happy. He had wanted to leave for so very long, from back when poetry wasn't dangerous if read by an unchaperoned eye and replied to with a touch of the lips. So let him go, she said almost confidently. He will see what's outside; it's the only way to get him to come home for good.

Aman Erum wore his bespoke polyester suit, so dark it shone, to his interview at the United States embassy in the menacingly guarded Diplomatic Enclave of the nation's capital. His heart was beating fast. He tried his best to focus on his suit, his new suit; it was the first time he'd worn it. He thought of Samarra, who would have told him his heart beating fast was a sign that he was afraid. She always knew he was nervous when his heart-beat quickened.

Aman Erum looked at the sleeve of his tailor-made jacket. It was a three-piece suit, a polyester-blend black number cut in the small shop of Zulfikar Sons. The tailor worked under a naked bulb in the basement of a residential building just off the bazaar. The shop was simple – just large enough for a client to stretch his arms out wide – but Zulfikar had a reputation amongst the elders of the city. Mir Ali's men trusted him to cut their suits, design *sherwanis* with Nehru collars for nervous grooms, stitch dark vests to be worn over *shalwar kameez*, and stylish leather coats for wealthier gentlemen.

Zulfikar advertised his expertise to both 'gents and ladies' on a brightly painted sign but, truth be told, he preferred to work with the gentlemen. When ladies accidentally visited the basement store, clutching their bags of material and patterns torn out of wrinkled copies of *Mag* and *She* magazines and Gul Ahmed textile catalogues, Zulfikar handed them the measuring tape and turned his back while they shyly read out their measurements. As Zulfikar copied the numbers down, he blushed.

Aman Erum had had no cause to visit Zulfikar Sons before. His mother had seen to the stitching of his *shalwar kameez* and the ordering of his school uniforms. But he had often walked down the stairs to the basement shop to touch the leather jackets. Inayat had one, made from delicate calfskin. When his sons were working men, he promised, he would take them to Zulfikar Sons to have them fitted for their own coats. But Aman Erum couldn't wait that long; he wanted something now.

Aman Erum had never bought a suit before but he had seen photographs in the newspapers of industrialists sitting, one leg casually crossed over the other, in spacious white and gold sitting rooms. They never wore *shalwar kameez* like the country's feudal landlords did. Their suits were dark and slimline, even though the industrialists themselves were not, and as they sat on gilt sofas receiving foreign investors and government ministers there was no question in Aman Erum's mind who commanded more respect. More than anything else, he had wanted to look like them.

He wanted to look sharp for his interview. He wanted to be seen in a suit.

*

Aman Erum had ridden from Mir Ali on a bus that carried workers and those would-be refugees like him, reaching Islamabad at four in the morning. He had been warned of the heavy security in the capital, of the circuitous obstacle course that travel to the American embassy would involve. He would have to present himself at numerous checkpoints and pass through the gated and guarded convention centre, taken over by businesses and buses that ferried ambitious applicants like Aman Erum into the Diplomatic Enclave, depositing them at the embassy of their choice for a fee of one thousand rupees. It was best to arrive early.

'Good! Get out! The faster you cowards leave the quicker we'll have everything sorted out,' the bus driver steering the late-night shuttle had taunted in Urdu. 'Hundreds of *jawans* – thousands – how many of our men have spilled their blood fighting you terrorists?'

Aman Erum had sat quietly in the bus, keeping his head down and making himself seem small so that the driver would not notice him. This was standard, typical. They had endured a lifetime of this abuse in Mir Ali – from government school teachers, the national media, policemen, soldiers – especially the young men. Aman Erum had learned to say nothing. He knew to look down and listen only to the drumming beat of his heart. The embassy had given him an appointment. He had his papers in order, his new suit freshly pressed. He was going to leave this, all this, behind.

'Well, let me tell you, blood will have blood. You traitors –' the bus driver turned in his seat and spat the word out of his betel-red lips – 'you traitors think we don't hear your music. That we don't understand the words to the songs you sing to each other. We do.' He bobbed his head over his large steering wheel. 'We know all the words to your traitors' songs.'

*

He walked from the bus depot holding his plastic folder – containing his passport, national identity card, application forms to Montclair State University, doctor's certificates required by the state of New Jersey, bank printouts and diplomas – close to his chest and tried to carry himself confidently, without seeming like too much of a stranger.

The streets were being swept clean by shoeless women wearing fluorescent orange vests. They tucked their saris into their vests and using *jaroos*, twigs tied together like anaemic bales of hay, bent their dark bodies to meet the grime and soot of the streets' gutters.

Aman Erum had thought that at least those charged with making the state shine would be given modern equipment, proper tools to make the roads gleam in the headlights of diplomatic cars. He had not imagined that the capital was cleaned by a Day-Glo army of Hindu women who wore their saris tied high across their waists to allow for quick movement and limber sweeping.

He had never actually seen a woman in a sari before, not in Mir Ali, only in the films he and his brothers watched when they were young boys, bootleg video cassettes pirated and trafficked through Peshawar. The wives of his father's Sikh friends, men who had stayed in the tribal belt long after waves of migrations had returned Waziristan's Hindu and Christian communities across the border, wore only *shalwar kameez*. They didn't stand out as minorities; nothing about them seemed foreign at all. They spoke Pashto perfectly, with no accent, and looked like all the other ladies in the town with their loose shawls, baggy *kameez* and loud plastic slippers. Aman Erum hadn't met any Hindus before. This would be the first time, Aman Erum thought, as he and the sari-clad sweepers crept along the forested outskirts of the capital like shadows.

He did not see anyone else on Islamabad's wide roads and

imposing avenues that morning, only soldiers nonchalantly manning checkpoints until the hum of the morning traffic woke them and reminded them of the seriousness of their country's security predicament.

Islamabad's checkpoints were different from Mir Ali's – there were no tanks here, no camouflaged shooters posted at significant angles so that anyone who tried to bulldoze their way through a checkpoint would be taken out with a clean shot to the head. There was no hostility in the soldiers. Here they picked their teeth with matchsticks and folded their arms behind their backs as they paced up and down pavements until a car honked, proclaiming itself ready for inspection.

At the Shah Sawar net café in Mir Ali a few months earlier, Aman Erum had sat at a computer after handing over his national identity card to the proprietor – a man with thickly rimmed glasses, who copied the numbers down in a large register before assigning him a seat – and searched the Internet for American MBA programmes. The walls of the café were brightly painted in playschool pink. Old ragged Bollywood film posters of chaste heroines with open, pained expressions covered the proprietor's desk.

The net café was crowded by boys, young men with head-phones, their eyes hidden behind dark glasses as they trawled through wallpapers of the new, bolder, midriff-baring, mini-skirted Bollywood starlets. But most of the screens, Aman Erum noticed as he clicked on pages promising low-interest loans to foreign students, weren't open on softly airbrushed photos of dimpled torsos or the toned legs of the newer hero-ines, but on embassy websites. They were downloading visa forms, copying down immigration checklists, and gazing at photos of Technicolor college campuses, replete with dewy lawns and sunny Frisbee-flinging athletes.

None of the men engaged in surreptitious Internet searches at Mir Ali's Shah Sawar net café ever spoke to each other; they never traded information or passed on website addresses to each other. Some walked straight to the back of the room, where Rustam sat, hogging space behind the proprietor's desk. Rustam wore his light-brown curly hair slicked back with pomade. He carried four different-coloured pens in his breast pocket and provided unlimited form-filling services for a fee. He had templates for the American visa form – no, I was never arrested on a charge of committing a hate crime. No, I am not now, nor have I ever been, a Nazi – as well as the British, Canadian, Emirati, Schengen and Indonesian visas. Any other countries cost extra. Rustam wasn't an advertised part of the net café. He just sat there unobtrusively, neatly filling out forms in his tidy penmanship while the proprietor signed people onto his waiting list.

As the young men filed in and out of the café, handing over their ID cards and adjusting their counterfeit jeans while they waited for the proprietor to point towards a computer, they sometimes exchanged a look or a slight tilt of the head. They were fellow escapees. They acknowledged each other only in passing.

Aman Erum sidestepped the women sweepers, whose wizened bodies bent at kerbs and announced themselves to the public only by the whispering swish swish swish of their midget brooms. He tried not to catch any of their eyes. Aman Erum was shamed by their work, by their submitting to this dirty capital city. He felt no compassion for their inability to aspire beyond it.

No one spoke to Aman Erum as he walked the desolate back roads away from government buildings and state offices towards the convention centre. Not the sweepers, who kept their eyes low, focusing on the grime of the wide avenues, and not the traffic wardens in their ironed blue-grey uniforms. But still the walk to the convention centre took him too long; he was dawdling – staring at the open pavements and the yellow chrysanthemums, the roundabouts, the roadside monuments, all named for the same few politicians.

When he saw that his appointment time was approaching, Aman Erum tucked his plastic folder into his suit jacket, careful not to bruise his papers. He wrapped his arms round his chest, mindful of his shiny new suit, and began to run. Aman Erum ran until the edges of his folder poked his stomach and his fleshy sides and sent a pinched pain to his lungs.

Panting and out of breath, his face flushed and his pulse throbbing, Aman Erum boarded the convention centre bus at six in the morning with all the other tired, harassed-looking applicants and they slowly wound their way around the slums of the Diplomatic Enclave towards the American embassy.

Aman Erum hadn't imagined the Enclave would look like this. He imagined palatial houses, grand embassies with uniformed guards and flags flapping majestically, but this was nothing. There were small brick houses, open sewers, barefoot children with matted hair chasing cars, men sitting on rickety wooden crates selling onions.

'Is this the Diplomatic Enclave?' Aman Erum leaned forward and, in his best unaccented Urdu, asked the ticket collector who had loaded them all into the bus and now hung onto the open window.

'No, no, no,' the man replied, his accent hiding something too – a northern lilt, Aman Erum thought. 'This is the back way. We don't drive in front of the embassies because it disturbs the *firangis*. They're out jogging and walking their dogs this early in the morning.'

The man laughed. Walking their dogs, he repeated.

When they reached the enormous white structure that looked like an obtrusively designed warehouse, the ticket collector herded everyone out of the bus and made them stand in two separate lines across the road from the embassy.

There were the immigrants who had come in familial blocks, infants and great-grandmothers shivering in the morning frost. Their smiles were weak and contorted, moulded into the same shape as the smile of the person directly in front of them: upside-down, teeth-baring, pinched. The families either smiled all together or not at all. The second line was of single men mostly, who were trying their luck as students, businessmen, but also well-dressed pregnant women with neatly blow-dried hair, who shifted their weight from one foot to the other as they stood in line trying not to look impatient. They were to be the mothers of future American citizens, after all, and held in their manicured hands references from Texan hospitals that promised they had the means to deliver on American soil.

The two lines stood across the road and watched the local guards in front of the embassy for a flick of the wrist, a nod of the head, anything that signalled permission to cross the street and ascend one level higher.

But the ascent was slow. Hours passed between one line snaking into the next and between the sound of the local guards shouting numbers that signalled entry into the next sphere. Snipers were stationed on the roof, positioned behind their Barrett sniper rifles. Aman Erum could not tell if they were Pakistani. The solid, serious-looking men patrolling the perimeter of the embassy, walking equally large German shepherds on tight leather leashes, leading them to ankles to sniff and to handbags to slobber over, seemed to be locals. Aman Erum watched the handlers as they passed by, hoping the dogs would not be brought over to dirty his newly tailored suit. Ahead of him a young woman wearing blue jeans and high-heeled boots smiled at one of the guard dogs as she chatted on her mobile phone. 'They're so cute,' Aman Erum heard her say in English. 'Yah, totally tall. No *yaar*, they're not Pakis. I think they're marines or something.'

Aman Erum felt embarrassed. The women he knew in Mir Ali didn't talk like that – provocatively, eagerly – not about anything and certainly not about men. Samarra never spoke like that. He felt his face flush as the young woman in the blue jeans carried on her phone conversation until a patrol guard with a dimpled right cheek and slightly crooked teeth came close enough to her for a chat. Aman Erum had been mistaken earlier. The patrol guard was white, a foreigner, but even so Aman Erum couldn't tell him and the woman apart. Though she was Pakistani, the woman in the blue jeans – with her indiscriminate smile and lazy confidence – seemed more foreign than the American guard. When she spoke her accent was almost stronger than the guard's, almost more American.

Aman Erum noticed that, with her high-heeled boots, she stood almost a foot taller than he did. He shifted uncomfortably, straightening his posture and smoothing his now-creased suit. He couldn't tell where anyone belonged. For a brief moment, standing outside in the cold, under the gaze of guard dogs and snipers, Aman Erum wondered what the woman in the blue jeans and her foreign guard would make of him. He was surprised by just how much it mattered to him. As he stood on the threshold of the American embassy, it mattered deeply to Aman Erum.

Later, having received his interview number, Aman Erum wound his way through the security check to the interior of the building, wallpapered with ageing posters of America's most wanted – young men with brown skin and beards so fine they barely withstood the repeated Xeroxing of their features – alongside bounty information written neatly in Urdu script, then into the fingerprinting room where he was given a swipe of cold cream to rub into his dry palms before submitting his digits to the biometric fingerprint scanner.

There were no heaters, but there was a television, tuned to a local news channel with the sound turned off.

It was curious to Aman Erum that such a powerful embassy would neglect to have heaters for its visitors, who had spent four hours that early December morning crawling into the visa section. His Zulfikar Sons polyester suit was beginning to feel thin, to collapse into his skin from cold and exhaustion. He had not listened to the tailor's suggestion of lining the suit jacket with some natural material. He thought it would make him look bulky, ungainly.

And so Aman Erum had not brought a shawl to wrap round his shoulders. He had thought it provincial, visa-inappropriate. He had worn thin socks, dress shoes, no gloves. Visa-appropriate.

Aman Erum wanted to show the visa officer that he was already halfway to America. But he was cold. He cursed first himself and then the embassy for its lack of warmth.

Eventually he reached the interview room, the penultimate room, with plastic seats strung in rows and packed by young men in uncomfortable suits, grandfathers, and single girls with hooded sweaters and nose rings, more demure, more sullen than the woman in the blue jeans and high-heeled boots had been. Aman Erum looked around for her, scanning the room quickly. She was seated at the front, in front of the interview windows, talking away on her phone and smiling at the embassy staff. Aman Erum noticed there were no heaters here either. But the embassy interviewers and staff behind their double-paned glass windows wore T-shirts and silky blouses. They looked balmy, tropical almost.

On the television screen mounted on the wall, a mute broadcaster flicked the hair off her face and shuffled the papers on her desk as the cameras turned away from her to an aerial view of Pakistan's mountainous frontiers.

Fourteen killed as US Predator drones strike North West Frontier Province village north of Bannu.

Aman Erum read the ticker silently, his heart quickening. He breathed slowly, waiting to see if any news of Mir Ali would follow, but nothing came. He thought of Samarra and tried to calculate how long they would be apart. He didn't want to leave her, but there was no other way.

President Obama says his country will strike terror wherever its tentacles appear. Pak President approves operation, confirms alliance to remain strong.

Aman Erum remembered sitting back in his warm seat on board the convention centre bus. Walking their dogs, the ticket collector had laughed. These people in the capital, the bus drivers and the ticket collectors and the peons, the girls with the hooded sweaters and blue jeans, they were anxious trespassers in the heart of their own country.

It wasn't like in Mir Ali; it was worse here. The army was both an invisible and an omnipresent force in Mir Ali. On the mornings of important religious holidays, you could hear their armoured vehicles squeeze through the bazaar, parking themselves at busy intersections, searching the dedicated throngs, just in case. Their black boots left large footprints outside the houses they entered in the late hours of the night, dragging out suspected militants to be interrogated at General Headquarters. The suspects' feet were never shod in shoes; you knew their footprints from the deep furrowed lines of disturbed earth, traces of people whose shoeless feet had been pulled, not walked, through the dirt.

There was no respite from the politics, none from the struggle of Mir Ali.

But these people in Islamabad lived on the periphery of their land so as not to disturb their guests. They lived as an aside, on timings that wouldn't ruin daily exercise or the scenery that a diplomat's dog might enjoy on his morning constitutional. Aman Erum hadn't laughed along with the ticket collector.

He had been trying all day to fit in, to sound the part, to look like an insider here, and now he realized there had been no point. He would never look or sound like them. But America was too important. Aman Erum would not be isolated by Mir Ali; he would not be held back by Pakistan. He wanted the visa too much. He would not be kept outside. He would work harder to fit in, to remove what was alien about him – his accent, his badly imagined polyester suit, his awkwardness around those women in the high-heeled boots and hooded sweatshirts.

Aman Erum's number, fifty-seven, was called non-consecutively, three hours past his appointment time and nine hours since his arrival in the capital.

Hungry and tired, Aman Erum walked to the glass window where he would be questioned by a woman with mousy-brown hair who spoke a coarse, heavy Urdu and who paused her rapid-fire interrogation only to slurp liquid from a large plastic mug filled with ice cubes that clinked together every time she lifted the container to her ample, unremarkable face.

Aman Erum answered questions about his schooling, his degree, his hopes for higher education in business in the birthplace of world capitalism, his aspirations, his under-standing of the American dream. On the face of it, he appeared calm. No one could hear his heartbeat behind the double-paned glass partition. He used all the vocabulary he'd learned in his B.Com courses to demonstrate his awareness of the American tax system. He confidently related details pertaining to his family background, his mother's maiden name, maternal and paternal family histories, his father's non-suspicious career changes, and so on.

What was the applicant's intended length of study and work in the United States, how many siblings did he have, what were his prospects for marriage, his reasons for remaining unmar-ried currently?

What did he think of 9/11?

Aman Erum lowered his eyes. He had mud on his shoes. He took a deep breath and tried to figure out when he had dirtied them.

Two aeroplanes hit foreign buildings, this is what people in Mir Ali heard. What they knew about the new war, what they understood about the events that turned their town into a battlefield once more, was this: those planes were flown by heroes.

But this is also what they heard: the wounded empire was waging a war against Islam. They heard that the war was a form of what the empire called infinite justice – it was infinite justice when they were the ones piloting the planes, but not when they were the victims of such just violence.

They heard that the men who flew the planes were from Saudi Arabia and Egypt, but that the empire was going to strike Afghanistan first. When it became known one October morn-ing, via radio and the local television channels, that Afghanistan had been hit and was in the throes of a foreign occupation – even though, it was noted, none of the men on those furious aeroplanes were Afghans – the men of Mir Ali understood that the state, Pakistan, had aided the attack on their brothers.

Pakistan had opened its air space to the empire, closed Quetta airport so that foreign soldiers could use it as a make-shift base, allowed them access to their intelligence files, and put their invasive agencies at America's beck and call.

Aman Erum looked up and nodded gravely at the visa officer's round face. 'It was a terrible thing,' he said. 'A terrible thing.'

How did he feel about the fall of the Taliban, she asked, between sips.

Aman Erum remembered Hayat, his hair long and uncombed, blistering with anger. Before 'you are with us or against us' was translated, Mir Ali chose a side. They were against.

'We men of Mir Ali knew that Pakistan would show its colours eventually,' Hayat had shouted at Aman Erum across the teenaged brothers' bedroom, where Sikandar was lying in front of his books. 'We always knew that they would enter the fray in a conflict so unprincipled and so bloody, just like they did in the first Afghan adventure in the eighties, only this time they would do it openly. With us or against us,' Hayat had scoffed. 'Against, against you, till we have broken you.'

Aman Erum had ignored Hayat's histrionics; his youngest brother was so excitable. 'Since when are you so anti, *haan*?' Aman Erum asked Hayat, winking at Sikandar, who did not look like he enjoyed the prod.

'Anti?' Hayat had replied, raising his voice, which had not broken yet. 'Anti? Aman Erum, they are their patrons. Who do you think made this the seventh-largest military in the world?'

'Fifth,' Aman Erum had said, stifling a smile.

I understand, Aman Erum now said solemnly to the glass partition, that we are passing through a dangerous time. It is unfortunate that America must fight this war, but we are safer for it.

With you. We are with you.

Thirteen days later Aman Erum received a letter informing him that his five-year work–study visa had been approved, with an addendum asking for one more interview.

Samarra's mother came to visit his family when she heard the news. Malalai offered her prayers for Aman Erum's successful journey to the faraway continent and handed him some money, a few hundred rupees, discreetly folded into a white envelope.

Samarra and Aman Erum met later, on their own, behind the Ibn e Qasim road mosque and walked together, contemplating the next five years. Prayers had just ended and the *gullies* behind the mosque were empty. A boy in a white *shalwar kameez* and delicate white prayer cap drank from a tap outside the mosque. After three sips, he lifted his feet from his sandals and gingerly washed his toes – a latecomer, he would have to pray on his own. Embarrassed, he looked away from the couple and focused on his feet as Aman Erum and Samarra walked slowly through the alleyways.

'It will be for our future,' Aman Erum said guiltily. He could not bring Samarra with him; that wasn't an option. She smiled and leaned against him. Her slight frame was bundled in layer upon layer of clothes, adding a cushiony bulk to her shadow of a body. She wore *churidar*, tight around her ankles, and had pulled her long hair back so Aman Erum could see her face. Samarra felt her heart slow down, the opposite of Aman Erum's – his heart always rushed with blood.

She spoke quietly, into Aman Erum's left ear. 'I won't miss you. I won't even notice you're gone.'

Now he smiled, careful not to laugh and accidentally bump Samarra's resting chin off his shoulder.

It was dinner time, the *gullies* were quiet. A skinny pye-dog, its mangy light-brown hair bitten off in patches and its ribs poking through its flesh, ran after a little girl wearing red plastic slippers. A window opened above their heads and a mother called down to the girl, 'Tashreen, come upstairs. Tashreen!'

The little girl in the slippers hid from her mother, pressing her back against the wall of the building so she couldn't be seen. She crouched down and stroked the dog on his neck. 'Tash!' her mother called from the window, unable to see her daughter beneath her. The dog rested his flea-bitten ear on Tash's lap. The little girl in the red plastic slippers bent her head down to kiss the dog on its sticky wet nose. Somewhere a sheet hung out to dry on a railing dripped water onto the street.

'While you're not thinking of me, will you remember that I'm going for us? So that when your father returns he will have no objections to our marriage, because he will see that I can provide for you outside of Mir Ali, outside of this place where we can't even sit in public for a cup of tea or walk our children to their school safely?'

Samarra stirred, careful not to lose her place in the crook between Aman Erum's collarbone and shoulder. She did not like the mention of Ghazan Afridi. She remembered Aman Erum loading the light-blue pick-up truck. Maybe years, he had said, before he got into the truck and drove away. Maybe years.

'I don't want to leave Mir Ali,' Samarra said. 'I don't want to walk on roads that have no memory of my life. I want you and me to walk our children to school on streets we know by heart, streets that have known us since we were children.'

She felt his shoulders sag, his back slump ever so slightly. She added, 'And I already drink my tea outside. Who can stop me?'

Aman Erum laughed, loudly this time. He held her face in

his palms. He told Samarra how he loved her and how he would love her in the years to come.

She wished that they could have married, could have signed their wedding papers before he crossed the Atlantic, but she kept her wishes to herself. Aman Erum's heart was beating too fast to slow down for anything now. She could hear it against his chest. He was on his way, finally.

The taxi driver punctures Aman Erum's silence. 'Radio says they killed three more today.' He does not need to specify who they are and who they killed. The taxi driver's inflection says it all.

'Where?' Aman Erum asks.

'At a checkpoint along the Atal Ali market.'

'Near the mosque?'

'On the way. They always keep an eye out on that *jumat*, don't they?'

Aman Erum feels his heart quicken. 'What happened to the soldiers?'

The taxi driver smiles, showing his *paan*-stained teeth.

'Our legions, *zwe*, our legions have dispatched them.'

2

Hayat sits on the motorbike for a moment; he releases the brake with his foot then pauses. He hadn't heard the rain this morning when he woke up. But now he sits under it, letting the drizzle fall on his shoulders as he rests his feet on the driveway. He runs his hands through his growing hair, hair he shaved off so early in the spring that it now curls in waves at the nape of his neck. Hayat watches as his breath leaves his lips and spirals up like smoke.

He kicks the stand down and flicks off the lights of the motorbike, battered and bruised from three years of Mir Ali's roads and windswept highway excursions to the edges of Peshawar's city lines. Hayat stands up and walks back towards the house.

His mother, Zainab, is still sitting in the kitchen, her cheeks resting on her palms. The gesture hides her face and her age, and she looks as if she is posing for a photograph of her younger self as she stares at a framed portrait of her late husband, Inayat, which rests on the sooty wall above the stove. The electric heater, three burning rods, casts an orange glow on her face.

'*Morey?*' Hayat breaks his parents' silent communion.

'Yes, *zwe?*' A slow light spreads across his mother's face as she looks at her youngest child, whose face is pink from the cold and the early morning drizzle. 'Your eyes,' she says to him. 'What's happened?' Hayat ignores the question. He involuntarily rubs his bloodshot eyes.

43

'Are you sure you're not going to prayers with the rest of the aunties today?' Hayat doesn't know why he insisted on walking back into the house, reacclimatizing his body to the indoor heat before shoving it back onto the motorbike to drive with the rain biting at him under his layers of protective clothing – a *baniyan* under his *shalwar kameez* and a warm jacket, one of Aman Erum's old leather ones – only to ask such a question.

His mother smiles. '*Kha, zwe,* I'm too old now to face the endless ups and downs of prayers every week.'

Hayat stands in front of his mother, running his fingers through his wet hair. When he lowers his head, almost touching his chin to his chest, a bead of water falls off the bridge of his nose. Hayat watches it land on the sticky plastic tablecloth.

'What is it, *zwe*?' His mother's voice breaks into the quiet lull that has developed.

Hayat takes his prayer cap out of his coat pocket and places it on the table. Who is going to wear this doily of a cap, a speckled cheesecloth of a cap, when it's drizzling outside? He walks out of the kitchen and takes a Chitrali hat off the coat rack near the front door, rolling its edges in his hands as he goes back to the kitchen, where his mother is craning her neck and twisting her old body in her chair to follow him.

'Do you think he will forgive me?' he whispers, leaning against the door frame, not getting too comfortable in case his mother answers in the negative and he has to make a quick exit back to his motorbike.

'It's better not to talk about these things,' his mother replies, moving one palm over the other as she massages her arthritic hands. 'Your father never explained his work to me, never really told me what he did or why he did anything. How can I advise you now, *zwe*?' Zainab nods to herself and concentrates on her hands. 'It's better the less I know.'

Hayat lets his body slide against the door until he is crouched down on the kitchen floor. 'Life is for us, we should stop living like corpses. We're not the same as we were seven months ago, three years ago. There is no other way. We keep fighting for the idea that there is another way, *Morey*, but there isn't. I don't see it. I don't feel it any more.' Hayat pauses. 'I've failed him.'

Hayat's voice is strong, his mother will remember later that afternoon. It doesn't waver or tremble but is firm and resolute.

'How can you, you out of all of them, believe that?'

'It's the truth.'

There's a brief silence as the cook sidles back into the kitchen. He lights a match and turns on the stove. Hayat breathes in deeply.

'But will he forgive me?'

The cook pounds dough on the kitchen counter, flattening it for *chapatti* with his palms, forgoing a rolling pin.

Zainab reaches out her hand, but Hayat's knees are too far away for her to touch. 'His mind was always closed when it came to this, you know that. I cannot speak for him. But perhaps there is logic to what you say. Give it time.'

Hayat nods.

'*Zoo*, Hayat.' She pats the table with her extended hand. He hasn't come closer.

Hayat only wanted his guilt assuaged when he walked into the kitchen, only wanted to be told: don't be mad, everything is fine. What are you talking about? There's no problem. He wanted her to say, 'Oh how sensitive the young ones are,' and for his mother to tell him that he was wasting his time and was late for his prayers. She only did the latter.

Hayat stands and adjusts the Chitrali pakol, a size too small for his head. He leans down and touches Zainab's forehead with his lips, grazing if not kissing her wrinkled skin. He wraps his mother in his arms.

Zainab laughs and moves her gnarled fingers to her son's

neck. Her knuckles ache as she strokes the hair on the nape of Hayat's neck, and she inhales the smell of the lemon soap that has dried and left a white residue behind his ears.

'*Za tasara mina kawam*,' Zainab mouths in Pashto into her son's citrus-scented ear. I love you.

Hayat hears her.

'*Wale?*' he breathes back. Why?

3

Sikandar is pulling the small grey Suzuki out of the driveway when his phone rings, vibrating in his chest pocket. He grips the steering wheel with one hand and fumbles in his pocket for the phone. The number calling is unfamiliar, lots of threes in it, no name.

'Hello, *kha*?' Yes? He answers cautiously.

'Is this Mrs Mina's husband?' asks the voice at the other end of the call.

What now, Sikandar thinks, catching a quick glance at the digital clock on the dashboard; what has she done now – it's not even noon yet. Sikandar knew something was wrong when Mina hadn't come to breakfast. He should have gone upstairs to look for her. He should have had one less cup of tea and checked in on his wife.

Sikandar moves his head yes, and then clears his throat to cover his ashamed nod and rebuild his authority with the man on the telephone. 'Yes. Is there something I can help you with?' He tries to sound polite, unassuming. 'I'm on my way for prayers . . .'

'If you could come to house sixty-six C, near the petrol station on Raj Hyderi street, it would be best.'

Sikandar sighs and changes gear, reversing his small car. The rain obscures his view as it collects on the windscreen. Cradling the phone to his ear with his shoulder, he searches for the switch to turn on the windscreen wipers.

'Is it possible to come after prayers? I have to make a stop at work beforehand, before the hospital goes quiet.' He mentions

47

this only to imply that he is an important man. He works at the hospital; he is a doctor.

It isn't a small operation – the two-storey Hasan Faraz Government Hospital has an emergency wing, an intensive care unit, a children's surgery ward, an ophthalmology OPD, and a maternity ward – but it is still being run like a dispensary. Doctors, the qualified surgeons and consultants who were Sikandar's batch mates and fellow residents, all applied for jobs operating x-ray machines in New Zealand or pharmacies in Manchester. They had long since moved on to more lucrative, less conflict-ridden countries.

The medical supplies for Hasan Faraz Government Hospital, when they come at all – when it is safe enough to guarantee delivery – are shipped from Balochistan.

There are pills taken out of their boxes and sold in strips with the expiry date scratched off the foil, a polite gesture from the Chinese distributor who insists on hiding what everyone already knows – that the medicines are older than most of the doctors. Syrups for the children congeal in their dark-brown glass bottles, and antibiotics well past their due date are prescribed to the old and infirm. The very word 'antibiotic' is magical. No patient who is prescribed them dares to ask what the effects of ingesting expired antibiotics at double doses might be.

Polio vaccines reach the hospital unrefrigerated, held up for inspection by some politician's nephew who has been made chief customs officer at the port. The Hasan Faraz Government Hospital has stockpiles of tetanus, measles, BCG and mumps vaccines rendered completely ineffective by bureaucratic delays, but they are relatively new and look good so the doctors snap their fingers on babies' plump arms and inject them anyway.

Nevertheless, Sikandar works at the hospital. He is a doctor. His medical credentials should have quelled the fast-spiralling

48

urgency on the line; they should have ensured that the caller's unceremonious tone was replaced by the polite respect doctors in Mir Ali were accustomed to. 'If that's an inconvenience, of course I can be there but if you think there is no immediate need . . .'

The voice on the phone, still nameless, says it is better to come now – the *dreham* prayers have not started yet and it would be best if Mrs Mina's husband could retrieve his wife before then.

He is already on his way, he says to the phone. Sikandar jerks his foot off the clutch nervously, causing the car to stall several times as he navigates his way to the house near the petrol station.

It has been nine months since this started. Before then, before the spring, there were no signs of any imbalance. The first time it happened, Sikandar had been on call. He had ducked into the staff room to take a small break, resting his feet after fourteen hours on the floor, when his phone rang. With no introduction or exchange of pleasantries, the strange voice of a crying woman on the other end asked Sikandar to come and remove his wife from her nephew's funeral.

Mina, who had not told her husband she had any plans that day, had simply risen after her afternoon nap and put on a white linen *shalwar kameez*, covered her head with a thin *dupatta* and instructed the Hazara kitchen boy, little Jahanzeb, who sometimes handled the home's vegetable shopping, relieving Zainab of the weekly grocery duties, and who was the only one able to drive when the brothers weren't at home, to take her to the address she had torn out of that morning's paper.

The obituary had been printed in a small square at the bottom of the paper's third page. There was no photograph. Perhaps the family could not afford the extra cost or perhaps there hadn't been time to sift through passport-sized photos taken over the years. It simply announced that the *namaz e janaza* would be carried out that afternoon at the dead boy's family home.

Jahanzeb, sitting in the car with Mina, thought she needed him because of an emergency. He could barely handle the car and drove convulsively – he didn't have a licence. He couldn't even ride a bicycle without falling off.

Once they reached the house of the recently deceased, Mina told the kitchen boy, whose face was patchy with soft stubble, that he could leave her there and that she would make her own way home. Jahanzeb assumed she meant with friends already gathered at the funeral, but didn't ask – he didn't consider such duties towards Mina as falling within his purview. He gladly turned round and drove back home.

The citizens of Mir Ali were not permitted by federal order to gather in groups of three or more in any public space, but the Islamic Republic could not ban people from sending off their dead with a Muslim prayer. Funerals and burials and prayer evenings became the meeting ground for the resistance. Even the dead were enlisted in the battle against the state.

As unwashed bodies were being rolled in their white *kafans*, men spoke in hushed voices of what was to come. Women, pouring tea from family samovars and serving cold almond sherbet to the mourners, passed messages under saucers and in the folds of two-ply napkins.

Even less appealing than minding Mina was the idea of getting caught up in the battle for Mir Ali. Jahanzeb had no interest in either. As he backed away from the house, he looked over his shoulder to make sure no one had seen him or noted down the car's licence plates.

Mina entered the house, Sikandar was later told, and made her way towards the dead boy's mother and father, identifying them by surmising that they were about her and Sikandar's age.

It was not an easy guess. The house was full of mourners, everyone's eyes swollen and red. But Mina knew what she was looking for. She strode up to the grieving mother and embraced her.

'I'm Mrs Mina,' she told her and turned to the boy's father to shake his hand, to his surprise. 'I'm Mrs Mina,' she repeated.

Mina then sought out the boy's grandparents, striding towards the shrunken and white-haired, adjusting her *dupatta* and announcing, 'I'm Mrs Mina,' while making the rounds among those she assumed were part of the boy's larger family.

Nobody knew Mina at this funeral; no one heard her name and flashed upon some shared history or familiar background. She was a stranger to everyone present.

After meeting the family and conveying her condolences, Mina sat amongst the cross-legged women on the floor, who were tossing burnished beads into the centre of a white bed sheet, counting off prayers for the dead with each offering. Sometimes they were date pits or uncooked red beans, but most often they were dark-brown tamarind seeds. Mina read stories into the sorts of people who used the different beads and beans. Only misers would use the beans, emptying their kitchen stock rather than going to the local mosque to bring home the seeds of the slightly sweet, slightly sour tamarind. Long, reedy date pits were popular too, but of course they had to be in season, unless the mosque kept a large supply. Among the stones, Mina had her preferences, though she had learned not to speak of this at funerals. She took a handful of the prayer beads and listened to those around her.

Women huddled together whispering about the boy. Karam, they said his name was, and Mina knew this was correct because of the newspaper obituary in her handbag. Karam's body had been washed against the wishes of his father, one of the women, a portly figure in a tightly wrapped chador, whispered.

The women clucked their tongues and shook their heads. One must never wash the body of a *shaheed*, someone said, speaking the women's disapproval out loud. It was his mother who'd insisted. She fainted when she saw her son's body. She couldn't bear to see her child like that, his skin blue and covered in blood and dirt. But still, it was wrong to have washed him when earthly appearances do not matter to martyrs ascending to heaven.

All the women agreed.

'I'm Mrs Mina,' Mina interjected. 'Yes, yes, it is very wrong. *Shaheeds* are pure beings, like the saints.'

All the women held their breath and eyed Mina suspiciously. No one had noticed her or her fist full of beads until then.

'Are you a friend of the family?' one of the ladies asked carefully.

'I'm Mrs Mina,' Mina repeated. 'Where was the body found? Did the police retrieve it? Or was it the boy's comrades who brought him home?'

The begums bristled. They were familiar with all the details of Karam's case, ready to divulge overheard titbits of family gossip and funeral hearsay, but there was something odd about Mrs Mina. Something too curious, they would say later.

But Mina was undaunted. When the women yielded no new knowledge of Karam's death and delivery, Mina got up, dusted off her clothes, placed the beads on the table and made her way to a group of youngsters. They were crying and echoing the adults' recitations of Koranic *ayats* calling for bravery and stoicism.

'I'm Mrs Mina,' she told the eldest of the girls, possibly Karam's sister. The girl was in fact Karam's cousin, and, upon being urgently questioned about the state of her elder cousin's gunshot wounds, she began to scream.

The girl's mother, Karam's aunt, heard her across the house. She was in the kitchen, where she had been helping to unpack food sent across from neighbours who had taken up the Islamic duty of feeding the grieving family during the mourning period. The aunt came running to find her daughter howling, while Mrs Mina stood in front of her, oblivious to the scene she had caused, tapping her fingers on the open surface of her palm and waiting for the girl to stop wailing and answer her question.

People took proper notice of Mina then and adults of varying degrees of patience and distance from the dead boy's family were called upon to get rid of the funeral crasher, Mrs Mina.

They took her into one of the empty bedrooms and persuaded her to give them her husband's phone number. They called Sikandar at work, demanding less patiently that he come and fetch his wife, who had caused a great amount of trouble on the day that Karam's soul would be carried securely to heaven by the prayers of his loved ones.

Sikandar raced over from the hospital. It was near the university, which was the only one in Mir Ali, and was where Mina had been a lecturer at the department of psychology before she stopped coming to work so that she could invade other people's grief and sit with crying strangers.

This was the first time that Sikandar had any inkling of Mina's new life since her self-imposed retirement from academia. He imagined his wife at home, in bed, under the covers watching Indian soap operas on cable television or cooking shows on the Pashto channels. Maybe she cooked a bit, inspired by the recipes on television, or perhaps she visited the tailor to get a *shalwar kameez* stitched, something warm for the winter.

In the car ride home from that first funeral, Sikandar hadn't asked his wife what she was doing at the dead boy's home or whether or not she knew the family. He was quite certain she didn't. He just fixed his hands on the steering wheel and drove while Mina sat beside him and let the tears fall down her face, dragging black tracks of eyeliner and mascara down her cheeks.

At one point he turned to his once caustic and whip-sharp wife and said, 'Stop it, Mina.'

Mina had only recently taken to wearing a *dupatta* atop her head, and she adjusted it then, a cloak she wrapped like sorrow around her, pretending that Sikandar hadn't said a word. She acknowledged only the noise that came from the cassette deck and the delicate voice of the legend who had sung to troops during the various wars the country had fought with its neighbour.

Mina pulled out the cassette, hitting the eject button with her bent index finger, and curled the light-brown intestines of the tape round her hand.

'Whose cassette is this?' she shrieked.

Sikandar stared at Mina.

'Now we listen to their musicians? To their women who sang morale-lifting paeans to soldiers? Whose tape is this? I won't have it here, I won't.' Mina shook her head, wagging the *dupatta* off until it fell round her shoulders.

Sikandar gripped the steering wheel tighter. 'Let it be, Mina. It's just music, an old tape – it's not important.'

But she wouldn't let it be, wouldn't let it hang between them unanswered. The truth was that Sikandar liked the music, he liked the lady's voice and the way she bunched her sari – it was always a sari – in one hand as she waved a handkerchief in the other, pausing only to dab her eyes in the black and white videos they showed on PTV.

Mina knew the songs so well that she used to hum the tunes to herself while she worked in the kitchen or as she read her newspapers. She had always kept an eye out for new cassettes. On trips to conferences around the country Mina always stopped at a bazaar and purchased the singer's latest compilation.

But now she could not be reminded of that memory. Mina lifted her eyebrows, tidily plucked arcs, and rolled down the window.

'Stop it, Mina,' Sikandar repeated wearily as he leaned across his wife's seat to roll the window back up, fighting with her to gain control of the outside world.

He needed a new car, one of those models with the childproof windows and locks that he could operate from the comfort of the driver's seat. Mina had managed to open the window, just a crack through which she could hurl the cassette.

'Let it sit on the road, on top of other people's garbage.' Mina was no longer shouting, she was snarling now, turning her anger at the tape towards her husband.

'Coward,' she hissed.

Sikandar dropped his head. Asserting all his dwindling strength over the rigid gear stick and tight clutch, he pulled the car over to the kerb.

'Mina,' he said softly, 'the tape is yours. It was your favourite.'

Mina stared at her husband, her eyes glowing, glistening.

'You always listened to it in the car; you know all the words of all the songs. You used to beat your chest to the music, like it was devotional. You said that you believed she wasn't singing for Pakistan. She was singing for us, for the small, for the forgotten. For Mir Ali.'

Mina's eyelids fluttered. She remembered the heavily made-up singer, her thick auburn hair woven into a bun starting at the nape of her neck and messily gathered on the crown of her head. She would walk to the stage in tiny steps, like Japanese Geisha girls or Chinese ladies whose feet had been painfully bound. The sari tucked her body into a curvaceous column, Mina remembered. She remembered her hourglass figure. She remembered how she had wished she too could place jasmine buds in her hair and sing of war and death as if they were earthly delights.

Mina put her fingers through the small crack of the window and gripped her chest with her other hand, beating her heart like she was resuscitating it. *Ya Ali, ya Ali.* She hit her heart and let her ink-stained tears fall on her white, crumpled *shalwar kameez*, and repeated the words over and over to herself while Sikandar drove home in silence.

That was months ago. Sikandar has kept his phone on silent since then, a quiet protest against the ongoing funeral invasions. The kitchen boy is sent to collect Mina when she causes a scene and no one speaks of the sari-clad songbird. Sikandar tried to keep Mina's secret for as long as he could, bringing his wife home and hurriedly sequestering her in their bedroom, locking the door and pulling the curtains shut so no one would see her wail and scream. But Mina's cries could be heard across the house. For weeks, Zainab stood at the bottom of the staircase, unable and afraid to make the climb, listening to her daughter-in-law sob. Upstairs, Sikandar would open the door only long enough to assure his mother that there was nothing to worry about.

'She just needs rest,' he would tell his family as they lowered their eyes uncomfortably at the kitchen table. 'It's natural, this kind of reaction.' He was a doctor; he knew these things.

Sikandar did his best to cover Mina's depressive rants, but he could not hide the funerals for very long.

Zainab started to receive phone calls, too. Women her age, friends and acquaintances, called and besieged her with stories of Mina's trespasses. Her daughter-in-law was crazy, they said. She should speak to her doctor son about having her committed. She was causing trouble and upsetting good families in Mir Ali. It was simply unacceptable. It simply wasn't done.

When Zainab told Sikandar about the phone calls he looked away from his mother and lied. 'She just needs rest,' he said, almost to himself. 'It's natural, this type of reaction.'

So now Aman Erum and Hayat keep out of her way. Zainab speaks to her daughter-in-law only at meal times. She does not call Mina to her room and she no longer asks her to shell pistachios for her in the afternoon. Zainab and Mina used to frequent Tabana's beauty parlour to have their eyebrows threaded and their hair coloured. Tabana had four girls who did the waxing and the hair ironing. She had even begun to offer Japanese bonding, a new fashion from abroad. 'Instantly straight hair,' Tabana promised. 'No more fuss. Very popular.' Mina had laughed and told her mother-in-law that when Tabana stopped washing her hair in the kitchen sink she might consider the adventurous foreign hair treatments, but not before then. Zainab now goes alone to the parlours run out of women's kitchens and living rooms, like Tabana's, that have sprung up all over Mir Ali. And no one mentions Mina's outings.

The Suzuki pulls up beside the petrol pump and Sikandar gathers his thoughts before he shuts off the engine and pulls his key out of the ignition. As the car falls silent, Sikandar listens to the sound of the rain falling on the car's bonnet. This will have to be over quickly. Eid prayers are starting shortly. He has two hours to deal with Mina, go to work and get to the mosque – if he wants to do so comfortably. Sikandar simply doesn't have the energy for a big fight on today of all days.

09:25

4

They meet in the history department of the university. There is no life on campus now, few signs of students or of professors going about their business. It is not just the university that has been snuffed out by the politics of occupation and suspicion. Mir Ali's schools have also been identified as dangerous. Children, free to congregate in schools and playgrounds, carry home news of comrades on the outside, their fates cryptically sealed in homework assignments and problem sets. Zohran and Zaviyan walk seventy kilometres together and then thirty and fifty-two kilometres separately. Though there is a fork in the road and some delays occur, both men will reach their final destination but who will reach first?

It does not matter.

A mark is given for the correct numerical answer.

They are alive, the boys are alive. This is the message sent and received.

There are maths classes with no mathematical precepts to be learned. No serious fractions, no solving of any kind to be done, just hope to be relayed.

But still the children have to be careful. Some of their teachers are paid by the state to report on subversive activities on their campuses and in the classrooms. Not many, but maybe one or two; no one knows for sure at the time. The teachers are asked to report on students who express separatist views, on those who talk freely about their fathers' travels. They keep special watch on those prone to boast about a brother's strength, an uncle's recent exploits in training, anyone who speaks too fondly of the great state's neighbours or mentions the years 1947, 1971.

They are encouraged to provoke students – young, old, it doesn't matter. All information is legitimate and hungrily sought by the agencies. Assignments, not the kind sent home in maths class, are written on the blackboard: What does Pakistan mean to you? An essay on patriotism handed out during an English literature lesson.

The question answered correctly earns the industrious student a star marked in red ink at the top of the paper; but answered otherwise it means something entirely different for the pupil and his family.

The university itself is small: a few low-storeyed buildings packed together, the various faculties separated by small avenues for bicycles and select, stickered cars to pass through. It is a young university, not older than its graduating students. Built by the province, Mir Ali's university opened itself to the town's aspiring offspring of traders and smugglers, who would otherwise have to study in distant cities. The education offered ought to have been largely free, but the province's weak funding and heavy corruption meant that only the district's wealthy ended up there.

The university is guarded by large wrought-iron gates. Over time they served not to let students in, but to prevent them from leaving.

It is almost eighteen months since the university was surrounded and the siege began. The students had been protesting the murder of one of their popular peers, Azmaray, a senior who had four months left to complete his degree in philosophy.

Azmaray had been tall and lanky, his hair growing past his chin and onto his shoulders. He didn't look like a troublemaker; he looked like a philosophy student. But he had been a threat.

Azmaray had been photographed at a rally, a demonstration in the growing slums of Haji Abdullah Shirazi Khan road, holding a photograph of his brother, who had been disappeared by the armed forces.

Askari disappearances. It was a service, Inayat had said, like termite extermination or pest control. The army had, of course, taken men and held them without warrants before, for weeks or even a few months, but they had not really disappeared before. There was a difference.

No one in the country waited for Mir Ali's missing.

It was the first time the national press picked up on the protests that were held weekly, staged by the Mir Ali families of those invisibly plucked and held by the state. The army, for its part, had been not so quietly disappearing men across its three border provinces – never from the centre – for the better part of the past five years.

Disappearances, there was a beautiful science to them.

First, they allowed the foreigners to come in and choose who would be arrested with papers and who would be transported over the country's borders. Young men from isolated frontier towns were taken to cells in nearby Afghan airbases and interrogated by young boys from Oklahoma. There was no need for the army to get involved then; it would only complicate matters.

Then the Americans took elderly bearded men, the fellows who recited the prayers from the mosque's minarets. But they weren't dangerous in the way their captors had been hoping for.

Suddenly, the army was eager to help out, to be a part of the process and to receive a School of the Americas training at home. You have to look outside the mosques, they whispered. You have to find them where they gather to speak of politics, of the war, of their allegiances. You can't find them in the mosques; they talk only of God there.

So the Americans let the Pakistani military in, wiped their hands clean and went back to fighting from the sky.

While the Pakistani army kept going on the ground.

Azmaray's brother, Balach, was a known firebrand. He had printed a pamphlet, a charge sheet, detailing Pakistan's crimes against its people. East Pakistan, Balochistan, Sindhis, Pashtuns, Ahmedis, the minorities. Balach had named them all.

Balach had been walking to the university, where he taught politics as a junior professor, when it happened. He left his house at a quarter past eleven and began the ten-minute stroll to the tree-lined campus where he would teach an Introduction to International Constitutions class to first-year students. He took out a cigarette as he walked and noticed the green Pajero behind him only as he cocked his head to light it against the wind.

But there were other cars on the road. Balach exhaled a plume of smoke and carried on walking. Twenty seconds later the green Pajero stopped. A man wearing a pair of finely creased trousers leaped from the back seat and grabbed the junior professor, forcing him to stumble and lose his footing as he was thrown into the Pajero's spacious trunk.

People saw what was happening.

Men driving in different directions thought they witnessed a man being bundled into an official-looking car.

Children begging on street corners knew what they saw, but pretended they had not understood the physics of a man's illegal capture. And so the street was unchanged. Life would be easier for those who had seen nothing.

No blood had been spilled. It was not necessary for uniformed officials to close the road to prevent passers-by witnessing official business. Nothing had happened.

When the junior professor failed to appear in front of his morning class it was assumed he had been held up with more important affairs, perhaps something to do with his family.

When Balach did not return home to his family they assumed he had been buried under a deluge of work.

When the next morning came and there was no sign, either professionally or personally, of the junior professor his father went to the local police *thana* and asked to file a First Information Report.

The officer laughed. 'Come back in a week's time.'

In a week's time the same officer acted as though he had never seen the old man before or heard of his missing junior professor son. His face registered no recognition of the case or of the time lapsed.

'Nothing to do with us. Go sort out your personal issues on your own. We're not a bloody complaint centre,' he said this time.

The police made no reports. They had no warrants out for the junior professor's arrest.

The military police suggested to the father, when he approached them timidly with stories of the dropped cigarette and the green jeep with the spacious trunk – stories that had slowly filtered back to the family – that his son had abandoned them to fight at the forefront of Al Qaeda's jihad.

'But he was a professor; he was not a fighter. He was not religious. He taught a class on the constitution.'

'Maybe he's run off with his boyfriend, then, *hain*, *kahkah*? He doesn't sound like a fighter, as you say. Maybe he's not capable of getting along with women and escaped to live a life of – . . . You say he's not religious, *kahkah*, look at what these fellows get up to when the fear of the Almighty leaves them.'

'Maybe he's dead,' one of them eventually said. If shame and fear did not work, not knowing would be their punishment. There was no final humiliation. It kept going.

Maybe he's dead.

Maybe he's dead.

But he wasn't.

There was no evidence of the state's hand in Balach's disappearance but that in itself – the lack of footprints, of witnesses, of news – was proof enough.

Azmaray, his philosophy student brother, marched every week with the families of other men who had been taken in the state's secret war. He marched with children who were cousins and sons and daughters and nieces and nephews of the disappeared. With white-haired mothers and cane-carrying fathers. Across the city's slums, around the marketplace, and towards the press club.

And one day a visiting journalist, who had been sitting in the press club's canteen drinking a cup of milky tea, watched the protestors go by and asked his colleagues what was happening.

'Happens every week,' they said, and shrugged.

The journalist followed the protestors; he took a cameraman from the club with him and photographed the philosophy student, his left arm raised over his head in a fist, his right hand clutching a picture of his brother to his chest.

Azmaray, the philosophy student, became a hero then. He became the face of the disappeared. His photograph followed the article of the visiting journalist who told the country of these weekly vigils for the un-dead. Azmaray coined a language for them, after providing the country with an eerie visual. *Laapata*.

That's what they called people like his brother, the junior professor.

The missing. The unknown.

Three days later, Azmaray, the philosophy student, was found in the middle of the small university campus.

His long hair, which was growing longer still and gave his wiry body the promise of a coming masculinity, was scorched off. His gut was bloated. His left arm, broken in five different places, was twisted above his shoulder. His right arm, the one that had been holding the photograph of his brother, the junior professor, lay several feet away from the place where Azmaray's body was found. His teeth had all been removed from his jawbone.

That afternoon the university held a spontaneous *namaz e janaza* for Azmaray. Men and women gathered on campus, praying together and weeping in their hundreds.

They were joined by families from the marches that Azmaray had led. The janitorial staff, mainly poor Christians who forsook their prayers in a different tongue to speak to God for Azmaray, came too. They all gathered to march for Azmaray, who was known, and for Balach, who was not.

That afternoon the army came and fired into the crowds. The fighters among the students, those who were leading their own underground cadres of poets and engineers, fired back. They killed seven soldiers. The university was set ablaze, the applied sciences faculty building was burned to the ground. Who started the fire no one can remember now. But from that time onwards the university was subsumed into a superior army presence.

At the gates, no longer guarded by private security, sat a truck of soldiers who checked every entrant for their papers. Another truck was parked in the quad. Soldiers roamed the small campus in pairs and the students who wished to duck behind a department for a kiss or a furtive cigarette did so now under the eyes of the military.

But still, the cadre that fired back met in the dark tower of the university's history department. Under the army's very noses, they hid in plain sight.

Hayat parks his motorbike and pulls his jacket tightly round him, fidgeting with the leather collar to stop the rain from falling down his back. He keeps his hands in his pockets for warmth and walks up the stairs. The department is housed in a mostly deserted dark tower rising off what was once a journalism school. Everyone in Pakistan is a journalist now. No one needs training to pick up a camera phone and report an edited version of the truth. The school has become obsolete.

For those students who meet in the defunct transmission tower, there is a system in place. They come only when called. They are never to loiter around the history department otherwise.

The stairways are vacant, cold. Freshly plastered green and white posters line the walls, all of them carrying the airbrushed photographs of a man sporting a well-oiled moustache. The day's date floats above his head. Hayat doesn't stop to read the patriotic exhortations underneath. The light drizzle outside hits the brown-brick building softly as Hayat turns at the top of the third floor and makes his way into the classroom.

A few students are sitting about casually. Some stretch out their long legs from beneath the haphazardly arranged desks, others sit cross-legged on the floor, their backs hunched over papers and notebooks, and some others stand by the window chain-smoking.

Hayat knocks lightly on the open door as he enters. One of the students sitting at the desks marks papers absentmindedly. The hunchbacks on the floor, scruffy young men, pass Hayat sheets of stapled papers, old exam papers, with brief annotations written in pencil between the typed questions. Their fingernails are dirty, broken and bitten off. Hayat rolls the stapled papers in his hand and slips them under his arm. The smokers by the windows raise their hands in greeting but don't move their eyes from the road beneath them as they exhale smoke out of the dirty window.

At the front of the classroom, she rests her body against the teacher's desk, her long hair tied loosely in a bun secured by two pencils. Her feet are crossed in front of her. Unlike the men at the desks, contorting and shuffling in their seats, or the hunchbacks on the floor, constantly rubbing their aching knees, she looks comfortable. The same stapled exam papers are behind her on the desk, but she doesn't look at them. She is commanding the meeting. She knows the questions and the pencil-written annotations. They are hers; she wrote them. She holds another pencil in her fingers and speaks in a delicate monotone.

'We've drafted the statement. It will be released a quarter of an hour before – none of the stations will even see it until afterwards, but that's how we'll do it,' she says, speaking to Hayat with her face turned away from him and towards the smokers. 'There are three questions for you, will you have a look?'

Hayat takes his eyes off her. When she speaks to him in the classroom he is supposed to seem detached from her, to keep his eyes on his notebooks and papers.

But he always drifts. He finds himself looking back at her. At her long neck, at her unpolished fingers that are always flecked with ink stains, at the silver thread she wears on her left wrist.

'One is simply not possible,' he replies, furrowing his brows at the first pencilled question. 'There isn't enough time to get Nasir out, even on a motorcycle. He'll have to go under.' Hayat doesn't look at Nasir, keeping guard at the windowsill. 'Unless you delay the release of the statement by a couple of hours to give us time.'

'No,' she replies swiftly, her head bent over her duplicate fake exam papers. She moves closer to Hayat so that she hears him in her left ear. 'We don't operate like that. We give them fair warning.'

Hayat sees her hesitate.

She doesn't want to give it. It comes as a flash of impatience in her eyes.

'Good,' Hayat says, looking at her. 'We're not like those animals who attacked the school van yesterday.'

'They're not animals,' she says coldly. 'They are fighters. This is a war.' She moves away from him before he can say another word.

Hayat knows that to argue with her is futile but he cannot stop himself. 'But they are killing children. They knew that could happen.' Hayat looks around the room; no one says anything. She pretends she does not hear him. Nasir smokes silently. He does not participate in the discussion. 'Children.' Hayat repeats the word. Nothing. She keeps her eyes on the paper, waiting for him to carry on.

'The second question . . .' continues Hayat, looking down and circling words on his paper with a fountain pen he takes off one of the unfamiliar young men sitting on the floor – there are too many of them, too many hunchbacks sitting on the floor taking up space – 'is done already. Should everything go smoothly, we will have people in Chitral by evening as part of the cover. His cousins, we said. Nasir is visiting his maternal cousins for the Eid weekend. The Chitralis are fine to go with that.'

She tucks a loose strand of hair behind her ear. She speaks to the boys at the desks.

'When can we talk to his family?'

One of the boys straightens, sitting up as he sees her swivel her attention to him. Nasir has become an abstraction. She doesn't use his name to spare him the difficulty of hearing a discussion he no longer has any part in.

A voice comes from a hunchback on the floor instead. 'The

better the operation, the later we have to put off the meeting with the family – to keep Nasir safe, they'll be watching every movement of the house, the family, the driveway, the phones. Hayat?'

They are the liaisons.

The hunchbacks will get money and basics to Nasir's family while he is gone. Nothing extravagant – some candles and gas lamps, because they'll have their electricity turned off once the military pinpoints where the hit came from. An old Nokia telephone to keep in touch with their relatives and friends is standard for when the military has the electricity turned back on so that the landline can be tapped. A small transistor radio, some money to tide them over while their eldest is gone.

Hayat doesn't speak to the liaisons. What has to happen to a movement before it lets in people like this? Spectators, they just sit and watch, ask banal questions, and keep notes on the members. Hayat remembers comrades, men who had devoted their lives to the cause of Mir Ali, abandoning their careers, money and families. Those men sat at desks all night and smoked and typed leaflets and posters and articles. They recited poetry because no one heard them when they used their own words. Those men, men like Balach, were the first to be destroyed. Now this is all the movement has left.

He feels entitled to his condescension. Hayat is, it is widely acknowledged, a superior operator in the Mir Ali underground. He has moved weapons, even heavy artillery, under the eyes of the military, taking rocket launchers through the very checkpoints they were to target. He has lured young military cadets to their death.

Posing as a young father frantic over a car accident that had harmed his pregnant wife, Hayat dragged the men off their posts and towards the bends and pins in the roads behind the forest. They had been persuaded to help him move the car, trusting his nervous navigation to take them to the scene of the supposed accident only to find themselves gagged and bound and taken as valuable prisoners.

Hayat has an honest face. Even those who do not know him, who have only chanced upon him at the university climbing the stairs to the dark tower where the students meet after hours, or upon his motorbike, even they understand there is something special about the boy with the hair that curls at the nape of his neck.

People believe him; they believe Hayat's sincerity before they have any reason to.

None of the other men in the underground have this particular power. They look contorted by rage, made ugly by vengeance. Their hearts are too corroded to present any other face. But not Hayat. He lives in the camouflage of his belief and carries out his services to his homeland without question.

He is a true soldier. You never see him coming.

Hayat looks at the hunchbacks on the floor. Their hair is unwashed, he notices. Purposely dishevelled. Too obvious. Hayat runs his fingers once more through his own hair and directs his answer to her. 'Yes, nothing if he's alive. Not for two months at least.'

She walks to the window and takes a cigarette from one of the smokers' crumpled packs before turning to Nasir for a light.

Women don't smoke in public; she is breaking form, bringing notice to the window.

'We'll take care of everyone, don't worry.'

Nasir smiles, but keeps his eyes on the campus below them, on the truck of finely suited and booted military police doing their early morning rounds.

'The rest of you should go,' she says quickly. The young men stand and the hunchbacks straighten their trousers and gather up their papers and their bags.

'Hayat, will you stay?' She looks at him, not around him or past him. Her green eyes are lined with thick lashes, long and curled at the ends. She has a beauty mark in her eye, a point of divergence from her iris – a wisp of dark brown that sneaks out into the clear white of her eyes and then, finding no room, retreats into the background.

She has broken cover. Now she stands with Nasir at the window, close enough so that his arms graze her waist and so that if she turns her head she can close herself into the crook of his collarbone. She will have to stand at the window with him for a few minutes, lingering suggestively, but she will leave with Hayat as per the instructions somewhere between the three questions on his exam sheet.

Hayat leans back in his chair. He is looking back at her too, not at her hair held up with a crossbow of pencils, not at her hands.

'I'm right here, Samarra,' he says, looking at the beauty mark encased in her eye.

5

There is a silence cast over the house. Sikandar knocks and rings the bell but neither sound breaks through to the living. He walks into the house and quietly down the corridor, which leads visitors into a large, crowded sitting room, its walls decorated by Koranic calligraphy in bronze and golden paint.

Glass ashtrays piled up with half-smoked cigarettes are scattered around vases holding bright plastic flowers. There are men sitting on damask sofas, speaking quietly to each other and exhaling smoke into the air.

Sikandar nods at each of the men, hello hello I'm sorry I'm sorry. He doesn't know who to condole with, so he meets everyone's eyes and touches his hand to his heart, I'm sorry. I'm sorry.

He does not want to disturb the mourners and ask who placed the distressed phone call, so he walks around the house listening for his wife's voice.

There are children, sitting placidly on the carpet of what must have been a receiving area for guests and less familiar visitors, picking at tamarind seeds placed before them to aid in counting off the prayers for the dead. The children look blankly at Sikandar. A little girl breaks into tears.

There are servants and bearers carrying jugs of lukewarm water on trays, their own eyes red and bleary, more from exhaustion from unbroken hours of mourning than from actual grief, Sikandar thinks. A pair of elderly women sit in two large leather armchairs in front of the staircase, rocking back and forth, mumbling *ayats* for the recently deceased.

*

There is no one in charge, it seems to Sikandar, who has little time and even less patience to spare. No mullah leading the prayers, no screaming women to meet those coming to pay their respects.

Sikandar pulls his mobile phone out of his jacket pocket to search for the number that called and demanded that he come to this address and remove his wife, and as he does so one of the servant girls, her old *dupatta* pulled tightly across her forehead, touches Sikandar on his shoulder. She has a fair, sad, moon-shaped face. '*Ma pasay raza,*' she says – follow me – and she climbs the stairs, two at a time, turning her head only to make sure Sikandar is behind her.

Sikandar wants to protest. He wants to ask the servant girl with the moon-shaped face if it is proper for him to be upstairs, in the family section of the house, on his own – a stranger – in the middle of this first day of Eid, in the middle of this house's most private moment.

He feels like an intruder. He *is* an intruder. The very worst kind. He is gatecrashing a death. Sikandar opens and closes his mouth, but in the end keeps quiet. It would be best to get all this over with. He follows the girl to the top of the staircase. She pauses, holding onto the banister.

'She's in there.' She points to the door past the large television set, sweeping her hands like a broom, ushering Sikandar inside.

'We didn't know what to say, we couldn't stop her. The family was so upset, so upset. Maybe it was a blessing that someone came from afar to take this burden off their hands.' The girl with the moon-shaped face stammers and stops, timing her words to Sikandar's footsteps.

Sikandar can't hear the girl any more. His heart pounds as he turns the door handle and lets himself into a cool tiled room. All the bulbs are switched on and it takes a second for his eyes to adjust to the light. Mina is sitting on the floor of the bathroom, next to the wide-open shower space, her sleeves rolled up to her elbows.

A young man is standing next to her, pressed against the shower's glass door, sobbing. There is a body on the floor of the shower, pale and stiff. Sikandar can only see hairless legs past his wife's frame as she moves dreamily between a sponge and a bucket of water. Mina is washing the dead boy's body. She has taken over the duty of preparing the dead stranger for burial.

'Mina,' Sikandar whispers.

She doesn't hear him.

'He was a child,' the young man whimpers between gulps for air. 'He was a child. They bombed the road his school van was on, his class van on their way to the governor's house to perform an Eid presentation.' He claws his hands across his face, wiping away tears that mingle with spit as he draws his fingers across his lips. 'The bastards thought it was a government car. It was a van filled with children. They saw heat with their sensors. It was packed heat: there were children inside. They fired an RPG into it. They didn't look at the day's visitors' sheet. They would have known, but they didn't know, they just fired.'

Sikandar looks at Mina; she is oblivious to the man – the boy's brother or his father or his uncle – standing over her. She is unaware of her husband trying to withdraw her from her task. Sikandar remembers Hayat mentioning the attack at the kitchen table last night. 'Have you seen? Have you seen what it has come to?' Hayat said, pushing the evening edition of the newspaper across the table. He blinked quickly as he spoke. 'Children. It's always children now.' Sikandar paused over his plate. He looked up at Hayat, whose agitation he did not recognize. 'Always, *ror*?' Hayat put down his glass. He wiped his mouth with the back of his hand and stood up.

Sikandar had become too sensitive; maybe as much as his

wife, he worried sometimes. Sikandar was glad she hadn't been at the kitchen table. Hayat and Mina might have been kindred spirits once. At one time they had been each other's favourites. Sikandar remembers how in the days after their marriage, Hayat used to greet Mina every morning by drumming his palm and fingers on the kitchen table, welcoming her with song. Mina would laugh and clap her hands with glee as her younger brother-in-law improvised the table-top music.

Hayat had been so kind to Mina when she was a new bride. He did everything he could to make her feel at home and embrace her into the family. For her part, Mina had doted on Hayat as if he had been her own brother. Now Sikandar feels himself increasingly isolated from their tempers and moods. None of them are the same any more. Everyone has slowly broken down over the past year.

Sikandar no longer has the heart to read the news. He walks away from television newscasts, which are on a twenty-four-hour loop, and from kitchen-table discussions on the violence. It's too much. It's every day, all day. The violence has started to follow you home.

'Mina, come.'

Sikandar pushes his wife's hair off her face, but she ignores him and raises an elbow to her fringe, like a barricade, to stop her hair from falling in front of her eyes.

She sings to the boy, reciting Rahman Baba's poetry to him in a soft voice as she washes his knees gently with the sponge, preparing him as if he were going to say his prayers.

I thought I could wake up this sleeping country with my cries,
 but still they sleep as if in a dream.

Mina bathes the dead boy tenderly, stopping her recitations of poetry only to murmur the *fateha* prayer over his head. She switches her tongue, moving from Pashto to Arabic, her breath blowing across the boy's face from his left ear to his right ear, so both the devils and the angels who follow him will hear the prayer and not stand in the way of his ascension.

'Mina, please come.'

Sikandar reaches down and grabs hold of her elbows. He will carry her off the bathroom floor if he has to. He wishes she would look up at him and acknowledge the madness of the two of them standing in suds up to their ankles in a stranger's tiled bathroom, washing the joints of a dead child.

Mina pushes her husband back.

'I'm not finished.'

'I'm not finished,' she says again to the boy's relative.

'Mrs Mina heard about Habib and came to us, she came to help us,' the grown man says to Sikandar, almost pleading with him not to take her away. He was so caught in his grief – he had been unable to wash Habib, his fourteen-year-old nephew, his elder sister's only son – that he had not heard the rush of voices through the house that wanted Mrs Mina removed.

She had been asking her usual questions. Where was the boy when his body was found? Where had he been going? Was there any official paperwork that notified the family of the details of what had caused their son's death? Was there any sign that the boy wanted to die, that he had chased his own death?

The young man hadn't heard Mina ask any of those questions. He had been in the bathroom, cowering over the boy he had watched playing cricket as a child, over the same legs that had carried Habib to his uncle, who had then hoisted him above his head, turning them both into a giant that strode across the cricket pitch as they pretended to be one of the gargantuan Australians who dominated that year's 20–20 matches. He couldn't do it, he couldn't wash those legs. He couldn't clean the knuckles on Habib's hand, his soft unworked hands, or bring himself to wash behind the prepubescent boy's ears. Mrs Mina found him in the bathroom, standing over the boy as the family waited for the clean body to be carried down the stairs and towards the graveyard.

She dropped to the floor, rolled up her sleeves, tied back her hair and began to wash the body.

The young man was anxiously grateful, but he could not leave his post. He did not want to fail his sister, who had been sedated by a doctor. He didn't want to forgo his last hour with the boy whose birth he had witnessed, himself not much older than the corpse now being bathed in front of him. He wasn't ready to part with Mina either, not yet.

'Mina.'

'Hmm?'

'We have to leave.'

But Mina will not desert Habib and his right to poetry.

I thought I could wake up this sleeping country with my cries . . .

6

Aman Erum shuts the taxi door, pushing his weight against the dusty yellow car. The office he is about to enter is a travel agency specializing in trips to Saudi Arabia, ferrying poor pilgrims to the Hajj on money they have saved and scrounged. Aman Erum turns the unlocked door handle and steps onto the pale-blue carpet that matches the rest of the office. It curls under his feet. There is no one else here.

Bismillah Travels is the only travel agency in Mir Ali, kept afloat by dedicated pilgrims. There are, at present, three Hajj packages the agency pushes upon its clients. The cheapest is the basic Hajj package, the village package.

It is the village package because only the city's villagers are too poor to have any other alternatives. They take loans on their cooperatives and pawn meagre jewellery – anaemic threads of gold necklaces or easily bendable bangles – to pay the thirty thousand rupees that would see them flown to the holy land no better than cattle: rib to rib on the cheapest airline possible (Ethiopian Airlines from Peshawar).

They sleep forty to a room full of flies and desert beetles, men lined up like matchsticks, feet to head and head to feet. The women fare no better. If they manage to hold onto it long enough, their luggage doubles as pillows.

Most middle-class families went straight for the mid-range option, Bismillah Travels found. They want spiritual vaccination against any future sins their newly expanding wealth might saddle them with. They have nothing substantial to atone for so just a spot of prayer, an experimental dip, does the trick, while the rest of the time the children run to Burger King, the mothers flock en masse to the gold souks, and their husbands smoke hubbly-bubbly water pipes in cafés and discuss how much their souls have been strengthened by the experience of Hajj.

The prince's choice package, on the other hand, runs for over a hundred thousand rupees and then some. Bismillah Travels sells more of the prince's package than you'd expect, considering the Hajj is a pilgrimage based on the idea of simplicity and equality amongst the faithful.

Business is so good that it allows the owner of the agency to turn a private office over to the local army chief. None of the staff notice the comings and goings of extra bodies in and out of the office. The Bismillah Travels team has superb Ethernet Internet connections, five phone lines, and plenty of space for those who wish to serve their country.

Aman Erum walks towards the manager's office. He does not want to attend this meeting, not today of all days, but the message that beeped on his phone along with the alarm bell this morning did not ask for an appointment. It announced it.

The office is empty; the staff has been given three days off for Eid. There are four private rooms, their doors pulled shut, while the rest of the office's semi-private cubicles sit in a quiet darkness as the entire office's shutters have been pulled down. There is no natural light in the corridors, only a dim phosphorescent light blinking over a rusted ceiling fan. And something else. Aman Erum stops and looks around. There doesn't seem to be anyone using the Photostat. And the fax machines are unplugged. It takes him a second before he realizes the glow is coming from assorted computer screen savers.

Aman Erum enters the room and presents himself.

'Good morning, Colonel,' he says, bowing his head slightly as he speaks.

Colonel Tarik's hands move from the steeple he has formed under his chin. He pats the desk with his thin, knotted hand and motions for Aman Erum to come closer. 'Sit, sit,' he says. 'Pull the chair round. I want to see you.'

Aman Erum lifts the small leather chair and brings it closer, to the front of the manager's desk that Colonel Tarik has commandeered this morning.

'Closer, closer,' the Colonel says.

Aman Erum pulls the chair round the desk till the Colonel raises his hand. He sits down. His knees, if he does not draw his legs as close to his body as possible, knock against the Colonel's. Aman Erum uncomfortably folds his legs, mindful that his humiliations have already begun.

'Tell me, *grana* . . .' The Colonel always uses honorifics, always speaks in their language. It makes Aman Erum nervous. He has not yet learned how to fully read the Colonel. 'How has your move back home been – you're settled now?'

Aman Erum answers carefully. 'Yes,' he says in a voice so tight it might have come from another man's lips. 'Thank you, I am settled.'

'*Kha, kha,*' the Colonel says, fingering the calendar that sits on the manager's desk. 'And your family? Do they thrive?'

Aman Erum looks at the Colonel's face, at his eyes weighed down by darkly lined bags and small smatterings of sunspots, and lowers his own eyes. 'Fine, thank you.'

'And that young lady . . .'

Aman Erum feels his ears flood, wishing himself deaf as her name is uttered by the Colonel. The blood rushes across his temples and flushes his ears with white noise. He does not want to hear her name on the Colonel's tongue, does not want to hear what he will call her, which language he will insult her in.

'That young lady, is she still causing you trouble?'

Aman Erum's eyes, fixed on the pale-blue, cerulean almost, shagpile carpet that springs and waves and waffles beneath his dark soles, close. '*Mafi ghawaram, saib.*' I'm sorry, sir. His eyes burn. He keeps them shut.

'Oh ho, don't be sorry, *grana*. These things happen. Our relationship moves past all these hiccups, don't you worry.' Colonel Tariq reaches out his palm and places it on Aman Erum's knee.

Aman Erum opens his eyes. The Colonel's left hand lingers; he still wears his wedding ring.

'There was an attack at the Atal Ali market checkpoint today.' Colonel Tarik moves his hand from Aman Erum's knee and places it back on his own lap. 'Three dead, twenty-one injured.'

Aman Erum pushes his chair back an inch, as if he too is adjusting to the new tone of conversation, making sure the move is not so obvious as to offend the Colonel. The carpet shudders when Aman Erum moves his feet, the tight blue curls retreating and responding to every movement of his feet. If you dropped a penny, a weightless copper penny, it would shrink for a second under the carpet's mass.

'It was a woman, did you know that?'

Aman Erum didn't know that. The taxi driver had been somewhat macho in his description of the soldiers being dealt with. Our legions, our legions have dispatched them. Aman Erum shakes his head no to the Colonel.

'She was young too, beautiful, from what we could still see of her. Tight figure, nice teeth. We still have her teeth, *grana*. She might have been a student, we don't know yet. The communiqué left by her handlers, those jihadists –' he spits out the word and flecks of his spittle land on the manager's leather diary – 'is still being checked.'

Colonel Tarik's hand remains on his lap. He leans forward. 'She didn't die with the explosion, *grana*.' He smiles. His teeth, in fact, are perfect, marred only by creeping tobacco that climbs round his lateral and central incisors like ivy. 'So, this is what we want from you, *grana*.' The Colonel lifts his hands onto the desk, clasping one clammy palm in the other. 'We want you to use your American education to bring back some information on who is arranging these attacks, who is paying for them, who writes the communiqués.'

Aman Erum nods.

'Where do they sit? How do they select the target? Why do they notify us beforehand less and less?'

Aman Erum wonders what military intelligence the Colonel possesses. He can't truly be lacking the answers he seeks. This is one of his tests, one of the common checks they do on their local sources every once in a while – a test of loyalty, of sincerity.

They know the answers already. They know you know them too. They know you can dig them up with minimal effort; you have friends and colleagues and students and intermediaries who believe that your commitment to your people is unimpeachable. They want you to ask the very people who would, once you had been betrayed as working for the state, denounce you. They want to isolate you from your natural protectors, your allies.

'I will do what I can,' Aman Erum says.

Today Aman Erum will give the Colonel a gift that he thinks will finally release him from their long embrace. He doesn't want to say anything yet. Not until there is no chance, not the slightest, of failure.

'Be sure that you do,' the Colonel replies.

Aman Erum steadies his legs, careful to avoid contact with the Colonel as he stands up. He doesn't want his eyes to reveal the information he withholds, the information that he has been holding and protecting. Unsure of what he is doing and unable to defend it, Aman Erum leaves the manager's room and Bismillah Travels with his eyes firmly focused on the crimped cerulean carpet beneath his feet until he hits the dusty pavement of Pir Roshan road.

09:53

7

Sikandar offers Habib's uncle his condolences for the last time. He shakes his hand and repeats all he has said for the last fifteen minutes, weightless words about patience and temperance in the face of grief; formalities one learns to parrot at funerals partly out of politeness and partly to give succour to the grieving.

Mina undoes her hair and pulls her handbag to her shoulder. Her voice is soft, still trapped in the music of the poems she sang and the prayers she mumbled during the pauses of her verse.

Together they walk past the servant girl with the moon-shaped face, down the stairs, out through the front door and into the waiting car.

Sikandar quietly drives his wife towards the hospital. He doesn't want to take her there. She will have to sit in the car and wait while he takes care of his morning rounds. The morning news has started on the radio and Sikandar quickly turns it off. But Mina doesn't notice the change in the atmosphere; she is still singing Rahman Baba's poetry to herself. He keeps his hands on the steering wheel, at ten and two o'clock.

At the traffic light the car is stopped and Sikandar is asked to produce his papers. He reaches over his wife's lap to open the glove compartment. Mina does not note the disturbance; she does not slow her song.

Mina only lowers her hands to her lap and her handbag to the floor so as to make way for Sikandar to extract the car's papers and their two photocopied ID cards. Something rolls around in Mina's bag as she moves it. Sikandar hears it, almost like a jingle. He is relieved the officer doesn't pick up on it and prolong the search to find out where the faint carillon sound is coming from. The young officer looks at the sheets of paper, checks the stamps on the car's window and waves them on.

Mina's sadness keeps her in a trance. She moves in its company, she sleeps in the surety that it will be with her in the morning, and she journeys from funeral to funeral in the hope that she might come to terms with what happened to her son.

When their son Zalan was six years old Sikandar would put him to sleep most nights. Zalan was afraid of the early darkness of winter nights and would curl up next to his father. As the day began to darken, Sikandar could be found reclining on a chair smoking his evening cigarette and talking to his brothers. Zalan would carry his pencil case and his homework and set them at his father's feet in the living room and sit there, working quietly, until it was time for bed.

If Sikandar rose to answer the telephone or if he walked to the kitchen to fetch himself a glass of water, Zalan would fold his book shut and follow him. 'I'm thirsty, too,' he would say, nodding at Sikandar, explaining his movements. 'Who is it, Baba? Is it someone for me?' he would ask, twisting the telephone cord in his small hands, knowing full well that no classmate of his would be on the other end of the line.

Sikandar never let on that he understood Zalan's anxiety in those months. He merely fetched his young son a cup of water and patted Zalan's bony little back, his shoulder blades too big for his small frame.

On his birthday they had bought Bubblegummers from the bazaar. The shoes lit up blue and red flashing lights whenever the heel touched the ground. All the children had those trainers that year. Zalan had worn the Bubblegummers home from the bazaar. He begged his parents to let him wear them to bed.

'They're so new, they're barely even dirty,' Zalan whined.

'Not after the walk home from the bazaar,' Zalan's parents countered.

'I will wear them until after story time. Just before I fall asleep I'll take them off.'

They did not relent.

'I'm scared,' Zalan finally said. 'The lights will protect me.'

Sikandar laid down a firm no and the Bubblegummers were taken off. But the shoes were sensitively rigged. Their lights did not die down but flickered gently on the floor. Zalan lay in bed, the covers pulled up to his face in the dark room, with the door ajar so he could watch the lights dance.

There is chaos at the hospital, the usual agitated mothers and angry patients demanding more time and attention from a pool of doctors who don't have either to spare. Shifts are being rotated for the Eid holidays and attendees have been left to pick up most of the slack, but Sikandar comes into work this Friday morning regardless, with Mina sitting in the front seat of the grey Suzuki in a daze. He does not want to bring her here. She doesn't want to be here, either. Mina sits in the car and doesn't move, doesn't turn her head left or right but just looks straight ahead. Before he gets out of the car, Sikandar turns the radio back on to keep Mina company.

. . . *Four hundred of Mir Ali's young men are expected to be initiated –*

Sikandar turns the dial off. They're still talking about the visit.

Sikandar walks into the casualty ward at Hasan Faraz Government Hospital this Friday morning before prayers, an act of charity on his part.

He prays only to keep the family happy. He lost the joy of the practice and the comfort of the habit many months ago.

He comes to the hospital to get away, to show his face – though he knows no serious work can be undertaken in an hour – and to wrap up loose ends. His shifts in casualty are typically eight hours long, minimum, without factoring in the ritual of haggling over payment with patients who expect free treatment at the shoddy government hospital. In the good old days, decades and decades ago, and good only for some, government hospitals provided nutritious meals to their in-patients, free care and medicine, electricity and post-operative counselling.

The explosion destroyed the blood bank, significant parts of the ER, and the processing lab. Scrawny cats now prowl the hospital corridors, sneaking in through holes in the damaged walls to scour for food. They make do with discarded placentas, which they eat out of half-open medical waste bins. A sour smell permeates the hospital. Urine tests are collected and stored at the nurses' station now. Visitors are instantly overwhelmed by a festering odour that no hospital-grade disinfectant can scrub off the walls. The doctors barely notice it any more.

Sikandar moves briskly between beds, surveying patients' charts and quizzing on-call residents about patient histories.

It is a slow morning. Sikandar expected an Eid rush, but aside from a few road accident cases and general winter-based infections there is no serious administering that can't wait until after prayers.

He roams through the wards, speaking to several doctors on his way, all of them scoffing at the morning's low turnout and promising a spike in carbolic acid suicide cases by mid-afternoon.

'The demand is too high,' the doctors complain. 'One has to fork out *Eidi* for all the children in the house and family, fifty fifty notes at a time. Then the Eid clothes for all the women, then the men, then the *daigs* of rice and stewed lamb that have to be served at lunch and dinner time.'

'Even I want to kill myself, ha ha ha,' laughs a senior cardiac specialist, who finds any opportunity to bring up his newly purchased Toyota Corolla, a luxury bought from Islamabad with who-knows-who's money. 'Maybe I should drink car battery fluid, too, *hain*?'

Sikandar slaps his colleague on the back. 'No such thing, boss, no such thing. Remember, *malgaray* – car battery fluid is, in fact, sulphuric acid, remember, boss?' Sikandar says. 'Our medical books called it the oil of vitriol.'

'*Nah, baba, za na poy gam.*' The cardiac specialist doesn't follow.

'Vitriol, boss? Vitriol,' Sikandar explains, 'because it's so often employed to disfigure women's faces.'

'*Kha, kha*, yes, yes, say no more.'

'No such thing,' Sikandar repeats, putting his hands to his lips and silencing the doctor before he becomes insistent about his imaginary suicide.

He leaves his fellow doctors and prepares to shut down. This diversion has offered a brief respite from what is still ahead. Sikandar stops smiling as he walks down the corridor towards the car, where Mina sits waiting for him, her *dupatta* pulled tightly round her head. He will drop her home, drive straight to the Bukhari street mosque and then back to the empty casualty ward, to ensure spending as little of the day as possible at home.

As he opens the door, his fingers moistening from the raindrops hidden on the plastic of the handle, Sikandar hears his name being called and the sound of heels clicking against the pavement.

'Wait!'

It is Dr Saffiyeh, a surgeon on call in casualty. She is a tall woman with short hair she sweeps back under a headband. Dr Saffiyeh squeezes her toes into modest pumps every morning, often to match the cotton *shalwar kameez* under her cold white doctor's smock. Somehow she manages to transcend the hospital's chaotic environment. Sikandar has seen her prowling the wards with several clipboards pressed against her chest and junior doctors trailing behind her.

'There's an emergency, past the forest,' Saffiyeh huffs, out of breath, as she points to an empty hospital van.

'Where's the ambulance?' Sikandar doesn't understand why Saffiyeh has forced this news upon him.

'Gone for prayers. All the drivers. Can't find any of them. There's a possible stillbirth – the family doesn't know what's happening, the midwife is some quack who turned up with crushed dung and chalk to feed to the poor mother in the hopes of producing painless contractions. Maybe the child is just in breach, maybe it's dead. You have to go and deliver it.'

Saffiyeh doesn't know his name, does she? She has barely acknowledged Sikandar since accosting him and inviting him to take on an emergency case while his wife sits quietly in his car. She hands him a small leather case.

'Plus, this is an ambulance.' She pats the old hospital supply van that has scratches along its side and a metallic Allah swinging on a chain dangling from the rear-view mirror.

'I can't help,' Sikandar protests. 'What am I supposed to do during the delivery?' It is a weak attempt, this playing of the *namahram* card, but he really has no time to spare this morning. 'You know what things are like now – how careful people are. How will they explain a male doctor?'

The brothers all have to be home to eat Eid lunch: freshly spiced biryani with soft lamb *boti*, yoghurt with ice-cold cucumber and mint leaves, milk and pistachio-scented rice pudding. He can still taste this morning's buttered paratha on the walls of his mouth. It had been an awkward morning at breakfast. His brothers had barely spoken to each other, which was strange since they had seemed closer these past two months. Hayat had been sullen; his eyes looked like he had not closed them all night. Aman Erum had been more than usually evasive and Mina nowhere to be found. Mina will probably miss lunch too if she takes one of her pills and spends the day floating in and out of sleep. If he is to keep himself Eid-free for the rest of the day, Sikandar will have to make it home for lunch at the very minimum.

'Who's asking you for your afternoon agenda, *zwe*? It's an emergency. Just drive there, correct the problem and be on your way.' Saffiyeh is all business. She holds her hands above her head, protecting herself against the light drizzle. The rain smells like dry earth, even here in this scarred concrete parking lot.

Dr Saffiyeh calls Sikandar son, yet he is – at least – seven years older than she is, with a light beard marked with patches of white hair on his chin and cheeks. Sikandar snorts, and while still standing in the lot he reaches into the van and turns the key. The van looks old. Sikandar will have to let it warm up for a minute. It sputters and coughs as it comes to life. 'I'm not opposed to heavy lifting,' he says, recovering from the slight. 'I work damn hard.' Saffiyeh pays no attention to him. She concentrates on the progress of the van's engine.

'I'm Sikandar,' he ventures, not having access to the inner workings of Saffiyeh's mind, which has already decided that this very sort of exchange is unnecessary.

'I know.' Saffiyeh turns to face her reluctant chauffeur. 'We know who you are.' She pauses. 'I was never able to offer my condolences in person.' Saffiyeh pauses again and studies Sikandar. But this is as far as she can go.

Sikandar nods. '*Mehrabani*,' he says, though she has not offered anything more than a footnote to a condolence oversight.

'*Zache zoo, baba*.' Saffiyeh's eyes are on the road, sweeping the parking lot before the van has properly warmed up or moved across an inch of concrete. 'Let's go,' she instructs, hitting the hood of the van as if to kick-start it. When it doesn't move she faces her new ambulance driver and raises her eyebrows impatiently. '*Zoo!*' Go!

Sikandar glances at the van, still sputtering and hacking black air out of its exhaust, and jogs quickly over to the Suzuki. Opening Mina's door he beckons her with his hand.

'Come.' His fingers curl into his palm.

Mina looks at him blankly. The handbag on her lap is pressed into her stomach, the way she holds a hot-water bottle against her during cold Mir Ali winter mornings. She does not want to step out into the parking lot.

'It's an emergency, Mina. They need a doctor. We'll be done soon and I need you to come with me.'

Having her there will comfort the family of the mother in labour. They will never accept a male doctor. Not even in a time of emergency, not in these remote forest parts. But Mina's presence might make a difference. She can talk to the mother, busy herself distracting the family, so Sikandar can get the business of delivery over with. Mina was once exactly who Sikandar would have hoped for in such a situation. Now he only hopes she will cooperate.

Since the funerals have been demoted to a fortnightly and not a weekly affair – they had been an almost daily headache back when Mina was manic, overwrought with the grief that now seems only to tranquillize her – Sikandar suspects that his wife is finally letting go. He doesn't know how she will react to a birth; he doesn't know if it will send her into a rage or break her down. Will it have the same effect as the funerals? He doesn't know. Sikandar knows very little about his wife these days.

Slowly, like she is being led, and for no other discernible

reason, Mina assents and walks over to the new vehicle. Holding her bag against her, she lifts herself into the van and tucks her *dupatta* behind her ears for reassurance, making them stick out clumsily. Sikandar looks at Mina. She suddenly reminds him of the early days of their marriage when they were both so shy around each other. Sikandar resists the urge to reach over to Mina. He hears the rattling sound again as she settles into her new seat.

Sikandar opens the latch to slide himself into the roomy front seat of the van and they start their journey, driving over the speed bumps and pockmarked roads that lead the way out of the parking lot. Chunks of rubble and charred steel columns lie where the gate once was.

Sikandar is careful not to drive too slowly and not too fast either, nothing that might attract the attention of the additional troops sent to man Mir Ali ahead of the minister's arrival.

Mina folds her arms on top of the bag on her lap and fiddles with her phone. Sikandar reads the address of the house-call several times to himself before he agrees with the directions, silently mouthing street names and left turns. He isn't nervous, his hands are steady.

The hospital van's windows are open. There is a chill in the air. Mina continues to check her phone messages. Sikandar mentally sorts through the paltry medical equipment he is carrying and wishes he had thought to bring more of everything and less of one particular passenger.

Sikandar pulls his jacket, lined with itchy sheepskin, closer to him. They pass the hospital's residential quarters and avoid the main roads, taking side streets whenever possible to lessen their travel time towards the sticks outside Mir Ali where a child is being strangled, born with its umbilical cord wrapped tightly round its neck.

8

They drive across the city on his motorbike, leaning into each other against the cold. It is safer for them to take small alley-ways, revving the motor as they weave in and out of narrow roads. In the shadowed *gullies* between ramshackle homes, children loiter on the streets. They drift around their crumbling neighbourhoods, fluorescent-green snot smeared across their cheeks, their scalps shaved to keep the lice and parasites from feeding on their skin.

Some have sweaters over their filthy *shalwar kameez*. Big woolly ones, ages too old for the children that wear them. The sweaters hang off their shoulders and cover their tummies like ponchos.

They stand there, in pairs, quietly. Gazing at nothing. Some of them carry sticks, tools to sift through the garbage. They are natural garbage-pickers due to their small hands and com-pact bodies that allow them to submerge themselves beneath the mounds of rot that collect on Mir Ali's streets.

Hayat slows down through the labyrinths when he sees the children. He doesn't want to frighten them, to rouse them from their glassy-eyed stupor. He feels Samarra's hair whip against his neck. He smells her, a delicate scent, as they brace themselves against the light December rain.

She wears a ring of *raat ki rani* on her wrist. A garland of jasmine flowers braided through a wisp of metal that she fastens on her hand. Her silver threads were once unadorned. She used to wear them plain, with the ends of the makeshift bracelet cutting into her pulse when she wrote or dressed and undressed, pulling fabric over her arms.

But that was some time ago. Now she adorns them with jasmines, like a bride.

Sitting side-saddle, Samarra holds on to Hayat. She doesn't say a word. Not even when they pause in traffic and make way for larger cars and vehicles to pass. She keeps her silence and buries her face against the back of his neck. It isn't done. Too conspicuous, Hayat always tells her when she touches him in public. It isn't done, even if they assume we're married. But Samarra ignores him, resting her cheek on his back as he drives. Let them assume, she always replies. But Hayat is discreet, as he has always been. He's secretive about things that are done and things that are not. No public displays. Not in Mir Ali.

Samarra doesn't drive a motorbike herself any more. Not since Ghazan Afridi left that spring, taking the Chinese motorbike that Samarra learned to drive on Mir Ali's mountain roads with him. Now she sits behind Hayat and keeps her body still, so as not to tilt the bike left or right, already unbalanced as it is, as they drive down a straight path. She sits behind Hayat and holds him, listening to the rain.

Hayat scans the road ahead, careful not to displace Samarra as he turns his face from side to side to make sure the alleyways are clear. He sees the green and white poster again. This one is loaded with text: 'Militants must lay down their weapons,' it says in Pashto. 'Choose to be a part of the tribal areas' inevitable progress.' They have no choice; they have to look at the proud army as their defenders and protectors. Hayat faces away from the posters.

He feels, as she moves with him, that Samarra's eyes follow his and that she shifts her weight, lifting and dropping her shoulders to meet the motorbike's subtle bend towards right lanes and left intersections. He wants to speak to her, to say something, something urgent, but she won't be able to hear him above the roar of the bike and the hum of Mir Ali's morning. Samarra does not hear well in any case. He speaks to her at a decibel he prefers not to, too loudly. But she can't hear out of her right ear. Hayat does not ask why. He keeps his silence too; there is little point speaking to Samarra these days. She seems remote, locked up by her rage. Hayat can't reach her any more.

He pulls the bike into a small patch of dusty ground near the recently scorched stadium and parks among the cycles and autorickshaws.

Hayat lifts himself off the motorcycle and turns his back as he waits for Samarra to straighten her *shalwar kameez* before walking through the parked vehicles and towards the hollow frame of the stadium.

Her fabric is a crushed yellow, embroidered lightly with faint strands of blue thread. She wears socks, navy-blue ones, with her brown shoes. She covers her toes in the winter, but not her face, not her hair. 'They can see you,' Hayat often tells her. 'It's dangerous what you do – not covering your hair. They recognize you.' But Samarra has spent a life lying in wait. She will not hide any more.

Not in any other way is she protected or prepared for warmth. Samarra drapes a dark shawl across her shoulders; she wears it as a man does, casually, carelessly.

She follows Hayat quietly, her feet stumbling over the broken earth beneath her as she balances herself, careful not to make too much noise but not to fall either. Out of the corner of his eye, Hayat thinks he can see her lips part, as though she's about to speak.

He imagines he sees her start and stop sentences, almost as if she were speaking to herself. Hayat has not let Samarra out of his sight, out of his eye-line, for years. Now and then he throws a glance backwards to make sure she is following as they walk.

There is a small semi-covered archway that remains upright, untouched by the machinery that felled the structure in which Mir Ali's men would gather to watch cricket or even hockey when the summer was good and the sun gentle. The archway had been attached to an annex that housed the relatively important entourages of the relatively important athletes or the very important state ministers and governors who came to be photographed on this rotten turf.

The annex had been demolished by the bombing of an unmanned plane. All that remains now is the entrance.

Hayat kicks at the chunks of concrete as he walks towards the biggest blocks. He doesn't want Samarra sitting on the ground, wet and muddy as it is. With the open palm of her right hand, she wipes the rainwater off a slab of what must have been a roof, a ceiling, a wall, and sits down on it, resting her long canvas bag by her feet. Hayat doesn't sit. He stands and struggles with his thoughts. It is quiet now, there is no noise around them, but still Hayat cannot find the words. Samarra speaks first.

'I didn't think I was nervous in the classroom. I didn't think it was any different to the other times we've met to discuss operations. There was no heating in the building – you know how cold it was in there, even more so with the window open and Nasir smoking cigarette after cigarette. But then, as I spoke, I began to sweat and I could smell my fear.' Samarra crosses and uncrosses her ankles.

She has forgotten how to meet the eyes of the men she speaks to. She looks away from them, her chin digging into her shoulder as she talks, her eyes fixed on a distant, hazy outline of something no one else can see.

Hayat senses a lull in Samarra's rambling monologue. He should speak now before she starts up again.

Hayat steps closer to her.

Samarra lifts her eyes from the wretchedness of their surroundings.

'Stop,' she says, looking at him for the first time.

9

Aman Erum met Colonel Tarik at his second interview, when he was called back to the US embassy. On that second visit a polite fellow in plain clothes, who looked foreign but spoke flawless Pashto, received Aman Erum at the convention centre.

He was seated in a VIP room, with leather sofas and VIP wafer biscuits and whirring fax machines, far away from the throngs who pushed and shoved to get through the convention centre and grab good places on the departing embassy buses. He was offered a cup of tea and his choice of chicken or beef patties while he waited, with his escort, for something to happen. Aman Erum removed his scarf and woollen hat as he drank his tea, sipping around the clotted skin of milk, and carefully broke the thin pastry shell of a minced meat pie.

They wouldn't have brought him back to refuse him, to rescind the work visa, he thought. That could easily have been done by post. Aman Erum had forgotten to bring a handkerchief and his fingers were oily from the patty. He was surreptitiously wiping his hands on his Zulfikar Sons trousers when a white jeep pulled up. It had official licence plates, antennae and a small uniformed driver. The escort informed him that they were ready to be taken to the appointment.

Aman Erum was not nervous; he wanted it too badly. He wanted to be free, to move without notice, to study, to learn, to expand his life that had so far been restricted to a border town. He had been quarantined in Mir Ali too long. Everything – success, comfort, respect – felt out of reach in Mir Ali.

He wanted to be a free man. He wanted a life that was bigger than his father's, one that came with luxury and comfort and choices. He wanted something better than Mir Ali could offer. He wanted the milky tea and the still-warm patties, too, if he was being honest. He wanted to be received at separate entrances, to be chauffeured by discreet drivers, to be accompanied by foreign contacts who asked him if everything, the tea, the patties, was to his liking.

The drive was short; they didn't follow the convention centre route that Aman Erum's bus had taken into the Diplomatic Enclave the last time. It was a few minutes, three maybe, before the white jeep pulled up at a small bungalow fronted by a patch of garden.

A white woman in a severe blue suit appeared at the front door. Her caramel-coloured hair was clipped short, curling over her ears and curving neatly at the nape of her neck.

'Come, please,' she said as she walked down the hall and into the sitting room. There were no pictures on the walls – it was a waiting room of a house. There was no sense of anyone living there at all. The sofas were a light pink, the walls a dull beige, the potted plants plastic.

'Madam.' A man in uniform rose to his feet as they entered.

He was thin. In his younger days his physique might have been described as trim, but there was no hint of muscle tone now. His scalp, balding on top, was lightly covered with strands of mud-coloured hair.

'Yet another one of your great potentials – how you find our best and brightest through your system.' He smiled and offered his hand to Aman Erum. On his left hand he wore a rose-gold wedding band. 'Colonel Tarik Irshad, *grana*. I've heard a lot about you.'

Aman Erum suddenly realized the white woman at the door

was not just there to let them in. That there was an army man accompanying her filled Aman Erum with dread.

Colonel Tarik's presence, Aman Erum quickly determined, was to play second fiddle to the woman. Whatever she wanted, he asked for. Whatever hopes she had for Aman Erum's United States sojourn, he expressed.

Aman Erum was a bright spark, they said. He was blessed with extraordinary advantages: his intelligence, his desire to fit in, his ability to cover up his accent when he spoke to officials and to lie low when he lived amongst his own. They wanted him to do only what he had already been doing. They wanted him to listen.

'Of course, you don't have to,' the woman said, shrugging, as she turned towards the Colonel. Aman Erum could stay here, in Mir Ali, they'd keep an eye on him. He was Inayat Mahsud's son, wasn't he? How had the last few months been for their family, since his father's illness? What had he planned to do with his life and his family's now that things had changed for them? Study, was it? Well, that's a luxury.

Aman Erum didn't want to hear any more. How had they known about his father's illness? Aman Erum asked the Colonel, his throat eating the words as they came out, why he had been rejected before. 'I applied, I applied to join you and you turned me away.' He fussed with his shirtsleeves, pulling them over his wrists as he tried not to sound too petulant.

The Colonel sat back in his pink sofa. His smile faded. He bared his teeth. 'Look at what happened in seventy-one,' he said, 'when those bastards mutinied and joined the Mukti Bahini. Taking our weapons and ammunition. They killed us with our own hands. Before we could capture them, they took us prisoners.'

It had been the largest capture of soldiers since the Second World War.

Colonel Tarik Irshad straightened his posture as he twirled the wedding band on his finger. 'But we are, are we not, extending to you a new hand, *grana*?'

Aman Erum made the deal himself. They didn't even have to lift a finger. He asked if they would expedite his student visa if he agreed, if he signed on to listen and to share the secrets he learned. Would he have more than nine months of paid work on his F-1 visa?

The power suggested by men like Colonel Tariq was more than those suffocated by it could bear. But Aman Erum was under the impression that he was different. Aman Erum imagined that he understood power. He thought he had cards to play.

Yes, perhaps they could do that, perhaps such an arrangement could be made, Colonel Tarik said, caressing the arm of the light-pink sofa as he replied, teasing the words out with every movement of his hands, the rose-gold wedding ring turning on his finger.

And that was that.

It hadn't even been a threat – it had been a question.

A note on a bio data form: he was Inayat Mahsud's son, wasn't he?

His visa would be swiftly issued; he would receive enough money to help him set up accommodation in the student halls.

But that would be it. This wasn't a financial arrangement. It was a patriotic one, motivated by duty not profit.

The Colonel would be in touch.

10:12

10

Sikandar keeps his eyes on the road while Mina fiddles with her phone, then with her bag, then with her shawl that isn't warm enough until finally she turns towards her driver.

'If you drive any slower, we may as well turn back.'

He lets it hang in the air between them. He isn't driving slowly. Sikandar is driving the way one drives in Mir Ali: cautiously. His foot lifts and returns to the pedal, his eyes repeatedly glancing at all the mirrors, dancing back and forth across the glass. He doesn't wear a seat belt.

Mina turns the shawl round her throat and repositions herself in her seat.

The leather of the upholstery is cold and sticky beneath her and she fidgets for warmth, squeaking her thighs across the seat. She checks her window to make sure it is properly shut. There's a draught coming in from somewhere. She winds the handle until it can't move. She looks at the small gap of Sikandar's window. Droplets of rainwater fly in, lightly touching his fingers as they clasp the van's steering wheel.

'There aren't any troops anywhere. You think that lazy bunch of conscripts will drag themselves out of bed so early on Eid morning?' Mina says, trying not to laugh, pulling at her shawl and flapping a hand towards the open and empty road. She can't help herself. 'They're still warming themselves in their barracks. By the time we get to the address, they'll only just have laced up their boots.'

Sikandar can't tell if she's attempting to make peace and have a conversation that isn't only accusations and entreaties.

He's had quite enough of those. Sikandar suddenly slams his foot on the gas and the van jerks ahead. Mina holds out a hand and catches the dashboard just in time.

'Is this okay?'

Mina rests her head on the back of her seat. *'Kha, za ista der mashkoor aim.'* So good of you. She laughs till black tears run down her cheeks.

'Der manallah,' Sikandar wheezes back, his words caught between his teeth as he laughs along with Mina, feeling light for the first time today. Any time, you're welcome any time.

Mina smiles and wipes her eyes of their charcoal smudges with her thumbs. On her fingers she wears talismans from her husband, her family, siblings, and colleagues. She twists each new amulet on top of a rising tower of rings. Silver rings with prayers written into them and semi-precious gems bulging from their settings.

Sikandar gazes at Mina as she wipes her face. She catches his eye and chuckles.

If you like their looks, gaze at them – she sings to him, displaying her heavily jewelled fingers over Sikandar's hands on the steering wheel – for once they are gone they will never come again.

Mina moves her fingers like the rain while she sings the verse.

Mina had always been the summer parent. Zalan was truly his mother's boy from April till September, singing songs with her in the car, brushing her hair when she got her comb caught in a tangle, and keeping her keys safe in his pocket whenever they left the house.

When there was no longer any threat of the winter's cold and its curtained evenings, Zalan would accompany his mother on her shopping trips. Or else he would follow his uncles around, hoping to persuade them to take him to the park. Aman Erum had never been very good with children. Even though he adored Zalan, the little boy was always careful around him. Zalan tiptoed around his eldest uncle, never certain when his mood would allow an expedition. But Hayat was the opposite; he never said no to Zalan. He seated him on his lap and drove him to the park on the motorbike. Zalan loved the motorbike, he loved the noise it made, how it throbbed against his ears and the way the air tasted on his tongue as they sped through Mir Ali.

Mina looks at Sikandar sideways as she performs, snapping her fingers when they aren't dancing, making sure that the ice that has been broken does not re-form. She feels assured of its thaw as Sikandar's foot drums on the gas pedal in time to her music.

This is the Mina Sikandar remembers from so many months ago. But she comes and goes in waves.

Just two weeks ago, Mina and Sikandar had fought terribly. He had had enough. After being summoned by yet another horrified caller to collect his wife, Sikandar finally decided to deal with this business of the funerals.

He retrieved Mina from the stranger's house and didn't say a word to her on the drive back home. When they pulled into the driveway she slipped out of the car and, hugging herself for warmth, ran towards the house.

Sikandar sat still for a moment, his fingers holding the handbrake. He turned the engine off and took the keys out of the ignition. He suddenly remembered he had to return to the hospital to deal with the rota of resident doctors. He placed his palms on his lap. He had to go in and speak to Mina first. He had failed before, on previous mornings and afternoons, but he no longer had the patience for defeat.

She was in their bedroom, sitting on her knees on the floor, in front of the morning's papers, scouring each page. As she turned the paper, her fingers ripped the edges of the thin sheets.

'Mina.' Sikandar stood behind his wife.

She did not respond.

'Mina,' he said again, lowering his voice instead of raising it. 'What are you doing?'

'You know.' She turned her face over her shoulder and spat out the words at her husband. 'You know what I'm doing. I'm the only one with even the slightest interest, aren't I? I'm the only one who hasn't stopped looking.'

Sikandar knew the choreography of these fights. He knew them by heart now. But he didn't feel he had the strength to keep up with what was expected of him.

'He's not coming back,' he said, veering off script. 'He's not with them, with these strangers whose lives you keep intruding upon. He was never with them. He's just gone.'

Still on the floor, Mina spun on her knees and launched herself at her husband, hissing spiteful, angry denunciations at him.

He was a blot on his family, she shrieked, waving her hands in the air of their bedroom. How was it that such a cur was born of this family? She was poor in many things, she shouted, but she was not lacking in faith even though she had to heave his disbelief across her back.

Sikandar watched the raw torment in his wife's mouth as she abused him. Her words got stuck in her throat; she was at pains to release them. He heard footsteps shuffling outside the door. Zainab. Sikandar hoped his mother, padding around the house in her slippers, hadn't heard Mina yelling. He bent his head forward hoping that Mina would quieten down, that she would hush her voice. But her injured wails only made him back down. He was unable to speak, forced to agree with her that he was wrong. He was always wrong. Nothing calmed Mina in this mood, not even that admission.

She pulled the hair off her face, her long once-black hair, now white at the roots and brittle at the ends, and pushed the newspaper that she had been clawing through off the pile, swiftly replacing it with another.

The presses often shut for religious holidays or national celebrations, but it didn't bother Mina. She stored and saved and hoarded newspapers for weeks and months on end. She eventually threw them out, after they yielded stale answers or directed her to empty funerals or anniversary prayer meetings.

She knew what she was searching for, though no one else understood. They thought she had just gone mad. But she knew that the only thing that had kept her from going crazy, that had given her solace, was to be with others.

She transformed herself between funerals. She had no other outlets or causes during the day. Once she had decided not to return to teaching at the university she divided her time by newspaper obituary boxes.

Families paid for the obituary boxes by the letter. A grainy photograph of the deceased, captured between tight black borders lined with grief, cost extra. Most of the notices were simple – a date of birth, the names of those left behind, a call to mourners to remember the dead with their prayers. That was all they had left.

These two on Tuesday, the *dreham* from Wednesday's morning edition in the afternoon, the death notices from the Sunday paper collected and saved for various points in the week. She had begun to measure out her days in two-hour slots. In the counting of burnished tamarind seeds across empty white bed sheets. In the memorized mutterings of prayers that moved the body to rock back and forth as the verses were repeated over and over again for the dead. Mina retained a certain calm at these moments.

She entered people's homes with a serenity that came with the feeling that she was closer to Zalan. Closer to finding him, to knowing what became and what would now become of her son. It was when she was removed, often forcibly, from those homes that Mina returned vengefully to the wounded woman that spat and swore and paced until she was let out again.

To look for her grief in the lines of other mothers' faces, to search for her son amongst other boys taken too soon, to know that there was a community of widows and the bereft who knew how she suffered: this was a comfort to Mina. She had not managed to translate this, to explain how it felt, but other people's understanding of her rituals was secondary. She did not lose sleep over their misinterpretations.

It was the hatred, the searing anger that robbed her of her calm. Mina truly believed that he could have been saved. Zalan could have been saved. There were many whom she held guilty for not coming to the call of her young boy's life.

At home she wore the same ripped tunic, its threads loosened at the elbows and the collar. She wore through the colour in the knees of her *shalwar* as she moved ferally on the ground between the piles of newspapers she saved for further investigations and the piles she threw aside once they bore her no fruit.

Her nails were no longer polished, though at Tabana's beauty parlour she had once favoured a silvery white. A colour, Mina said, like the snow on the Himalayas.

She did not think about things like that now. She no longer wore more than a rim of gun-black kohl round her eyes. She bought the kohl in the market, sold in matchboxes whose sticks had been dipped in the strong black powder for easy one-time application.

She kept them on a table in the bathroom, discarding the matchsticks whose kohl had smudged down the head and those with visible splinters. It was a village tradition, one she had carried with her since she was a girl, never trading in the cheaply bought matchboxes for the popular new eyeliners that came in bright blue and red sticks with detachable tops and mirrors glued on the side.

She did not look like, nor dress like, nor carry any semblance of the woman she had always been.

Sikandar had heard this argument before. He had been howled and wailed and snarled at when he made the early mistake of questioning her. He had seen his wife's hands tremble with conviction, her eyes blink and blink back tears, her voice falter with the deep need for her husband to believe her, to be on her side. To know that she was as close to finding Zalan as they had been in the year since they lost him.

Sikandar kneeled then, balancing himself on his haunches next to Mina's discarded newspapers. 'He's not coming back,' he repeated, moving his body closer to hers so that this time she would not have the rustle of the papers to camouflage what he was saying. He spoke loudly, a notch or two above the apologetic whisper in which he had previously spoken to his wife. Sikandar felt his breath leave his mouth. There was gravel in his voice.

'He is gone, Mina.'

Driving now into the forest, Sikandar no longer feels annoyed about the disruption to his day. He feels only hunger pangs knocking lightly on his stomach. But he ignores them and laughs and sings with Mina as he drives.

This detour has knocked Mina out of her slump. Sikandar begins to pinpoint moments of recovery. He realizes he had previously mistaken them for signals of further worry. But now, looking back, Sikandar hopes that these flare-ups – today's funeral, the fidgeting unhappily with the handbag and the constant checking of the phone – are the death throes of Mina's grief. Cumulatively, they add up, Sikandar thinks.

He feels ashamed of how he confronted Mina two weeks earlier.

Today Sikandar has not spoken to her in anger. He did not speak down to her in the car as they left the funeral. He had shaken her too hard last time. She knew; he knew she did. That was enough for him.

He drives while Mina sings and shifts about in her squeaky seat. She forgets the rest of the song, but substitutes the missing words with the poetry of Ghani Khan.

> But show me just this one thing, my darling,
> I seek a heart stained like a poppy flower.

They do not know the remaining poem by heart, so they sing the words they do know over the Mir Ali landscape that pulls them out of the city and into the poor outer settlements.

Other parts of Mir Ali, even the townships, have had morning facelifts – men carting small carnival rides park their four-seater swing sets and slides outside even the poorest areas and sell turns to the neighbourhood children for two rupees. But outside these newly crowded refugee camps there are no strangers setting up festivities for the days of Eid ahead.

They pass by the slums on Haji Abdullah Shirazi Khan road: small, bare homes made of rickety shingles with no Eid lights adorning the rooftops.

The hospital supply van, its windows tightly shut except for one, drives out of Mir Ali, past *chaikhanas* packed with men nursing steaming cups of cardamom-scented tea, and the dried-fruit vendor and his misshapen jute bags.

Men sit on motorcycles, thick scarves wrapped round their faces against the morning's light rain. They accelerate their engines and let their exhausts burst with a sound that reminds the innocent of firecrackers. Young girls dressed in glossy new *shalwar kameez* peep out of alleyways, their thin lips painted with purple lipstick and their brows knitted together by small *bindis* in deep plum colours or the new garish neon designs that match their holiday outfits. Even the town's transvestites, burly men whose muscled arms strain through their *kameez*, walk along the damp roads of Mir Ali, arm in arm, clapping their hands and asking passing cars for alms that will shower the generous with Eid blessings.

But the roads beyond Mir Ali are wild. They open up to the northern frontier with miles of pine forest and rocky terrain. Mir Ali had once moved with the tremors of its time, swaying almost – but not quite – to the rhythm of forest reeds. It had nestled shepherds and woodsmen and had been the home of mendicant princes and holy sages. Its people had been ordinary men who lived amongst saints and sovereigns. Mir Ali had been like this once.

But those who knew the enchanting un-kingdom, and those who loved it, watched as waves came and conquered and as partitions made and unmade Mir Ali.

Now many men live on the margins of Mir Ali.

Besides the woodsmen, there are the timber thieves, the gypsies, families living in squalor who warm themselves over open fires and dress their children in rags. There are the throw-aways, the stowaways, the forgotten refugees. And then there are those who hide amongst the miserable, men who prey on the desolate and the deprived. Those men hunt for acceptance, feeding off the discarded populations of the periphery. They are strangers amongst their own.

*

Mina has not laughed like this in months. Sikandar hasn't seen Mina's face sustain a smile for this length of time since it happened. But before, before all that, she had always been like this.

She would click her fingers to the sound of music anywhere. She sang along with the jingle of bicycles as children raced past the front gate on their way to the empty plot nearby to play cricket. Mina used to encourage Jahanzeb, the Hazara kitchen boy, who had a delicate falsetto, to sing while they chopped onions and ground green chillies, and she would tap the splintering kitchen counter with her knife to keep the beat.

The music had been the first to go.

The colours have muted since they left the city's main roads, the crowds have thinned and it has grown quieter.

There is something beautiful about the day, something Sikandar hadn't expected. Something has shifted. The light has lifted through the early morning December fog.

Sikandar is completely absorbed in the moment, by the sight of the clearing view and the sound of Mina's voice, just seconds before the Hasan Faraz Government Hospital supply van is stopped.

II

Aman Erum adjusted surprisingly well to his new continent. After a journey that dragged on for over two days, the cheapest ticket and the most inspired that Bismillah Travels could come up with, Aman Erum felt that he had never been further from Mir Ali.

He hadn't, of course. But to leave home was one thing and to leave it on Bismillah Travels' budget itinerary was quite another thing altogether. First, Aman Erum flew from Peshawar to Doha – where he walked between duty-free perfume counters that bore no trace of Peshawar airport's body odours and where he first wondered how it was that people travelled beyond airports when there was plenty to keep them occupied inside their fluorescently lit terminals; to Amman – where he burned his tongue on a thimble of Arabic coffee; to London – where he first encountered the misery of a Western toilet with its roll of toilet paper in the place of a *lota* and walked on moving floors, oppressed by a feeling of uncleanliness, until his feet carried him onto a Swiss Air flight; to Zurich – where he would wait almost half a day until he was interrogated by a large blond man who seemed at pains to extract the precise reason for his travel to the United States before waving him through so he could take his place in another seat that was so small it folded his spine in half, right over his un-halal dinner tray.

By the time he finally reached New Jersey, Aman Erum felt he had left all traces of Mir Ali behind. He did not walk with his head bowed. He looked officials – especially officials – straight in the eye.

He abandoned his accent at immigration. He had been tweaking and amending it over the years, fine-tuning his vowels, sterilizing his inflections. Aman Erum had not come this far to carry Mir Ali with him. He dropped his country like a weight off his back. In a matter of weeks he was telling those who asked that he was a student from India or Dubai, testing out which of the two was more believable. People believed both. Aman Erum never corrected anyone. He cut his hair, bought fleece sweaters from a second-hand store, acquainted himself with toilet paper, read books off the shelves at Montclair's independent bookstores, ate at Chinese restaurants and shopped at Korean markets.

Aman Erum's work–study visa allowed him employment at the admissions office five days a week. In order to fund his time in New Jersey, Aman Erum had to work twice as hard as he studied. He stood behind a chest-high desk – always stood – and filed receipts, stamped signatures on official correspondence and stuffed envelopes for hours every morning. He was unused to the dullness of the work. In Mir Ali he consigned such trivial tasks to a younger sibling. But here in America, he was realizing, hard work was everything. It meant mobility.

He watched the women in the admissions office; he saw how a Jamaican assistant dean with a barely decipherable accent scolded a secretary for minor infractions. Aman Erum understood how low the bottom was and how rapid the ascent. Aman Erum would best the assistant dean. In a matter of months he would mimic her patois for his floor mates, who remembered her from her garbled Orientation welcome speech. No amount of mean work would deter him from his foreign dream. Aman Erum was an escapee.

He saved money by reading his textbooks at the library. He would spend his days and nights free from classes there, an alarm clock beside him and a thin *razai* that his mother had packed into his suitcase draped across his shoulders as he bent his body over a desk in the stacks and studied. The light was dim but the sound of students chattering away on mobile phones carried on through the night.

Some nights he rolled up the *razai* and placed it between his head and the desk and slept for an hour or two. He had been given student accommodation but it was so expensive he considered asking for a term's refund on housing and making do in the stacks, living quietly and unobtrusively under the desks on which he worked.

Some of the Pakistanis who had come on science scholarships and year-abroad programmes, and were too foreign and too self-involved to pay attention to Pakistani politics, didn't realize that Aman Erum did not consider himself among them. They immediately recognized him as similar, as one of their own. They didn't buy the disguise. His new inflections and studied mannerisms did nothing to dissuade them from seeking him out. They often approached him to ask if he wanted to join their Muslim Students Association. He politely declined, saying he had too much work.

They invited him to *iftar* during the month of Ramadan and promised him preferential housing if he joined up with four or five of them who were in the process of applying for funding from a Pakistani Students Housing scheme. The food would be halal, they promised, the toilets equipped with *lotas*, and the bedrooms constructed so that one's door faced eastward towards Mecca for easier prayers. Naturally, the sexes would be properly segregated and watched over by righteous brothers and sisters serving as resident assistants and hall monitors.

Politely, Aman Erum always refused. He had no problem

with non-segregated living. Over time, Aman Erum's awkwardness around women in blue jeans waned and Montclair began to feel like home. He liked living in Bohn Hall, on the twelfth floor. He'd never been around so many different people. The self-possessed girls on his floor reminded him of Samarra. They were strong and independent and never put up with his nonsense. Adriana was from New Jersey but had family in Puerto Rico. She and her room-mate, Panthea Denopolous, a first-year student from Greece whose name Aman Erum practised and practised but could never say properly, opting to call her by her initials instead, were his first friends. Adriana chose Aman Erum for her team during a friendly game of Bohn Hall touch football during Orientation. He had never played the game before. 'Fresh off the boat,' she called him. 'Fresh off the boat, it's simple. We're all receivers. There are no running backs.' Aman Erum just stared at her. He hadn't understood a word of what she said. But by his first Thanksgiving, Aman Erum knew all the rules of the game and had a favourite team in time for the Super Bowl.

PD wasn't as athletic as her room-mate. She was new to America too, and she and Aman Erum took their letters to the post office together and stood in the interminable queues to send home a few lines scribbled on a postcard. In trying to explain where her country was to the postal clerks, PD didn't face the trouble Aman Erum did when it was his turn, but she always waited patiently for him while he licked and stuck his two rows of stamps on every letter home to Samarra. 'First in, last out,' she would say about their adventures to the post office.

Adriana and PD never babied Aman Erum but left his dirty dishes outside his room when he forgot to clean them in the sink. They taught him how to cheat the laundry machines and how to shut the smoke detectors without sending the alarms into their panicked default settings. Aman Erum told them about Samarra and PD commiserated with him over the loneliness of long-distance relationships. When Aman Erum got stuck working at the admissions office, PD would take his post along with hers and stand in line with his love letters to Samarra.

These were his friends in Montclair.

Aman Erum had not come this far to be so close to Pakistanis and he viewed their constant interest in him with suspicion. Who knew how many of them had received their visas with one extra year over the standard four arranged as a bonus by mysterious American ladies?

Aman Erum had no friends from his summers in Chitral; he had no acquaintances from outside Mir Ali like Hayat did. He did not know which one of the Pakistanis in Montclair approached him out of kindness and which one of them had an ulterior agenda. But he supposed that they all had, as he did, an agenda of some kind.

He sometimes ate at the cafeteria with the Bangladeshi students, whose language he didn't understand, but who nodded knowingly when he carefully and quietly allowed himself to speak of Mir Ali. They invited him to join them at meal times and spoke in English for his benefit as they complained about the dryness of the fish and the lack of sugar in the fruits, which all tasted of banana in this strange country. Aman Erum felt comfortable among them.

He knew that it would be said by the Pakistanis that he was a self-hater, that he had preferred to dine with Bingos and Hindus rather than with his own kind. They would murmur that their parents had been right. There was something strange about these northerners and their inability to fit in, they would say, but Aman Erum didn't care.

He had never met anyone else who understood what he and

his brothers had known, what all their friends and their parents' friends had spoken about in hushed tones at wedding parties and late-night dinners in living rooms – that there was an injustice that was swallowing their people whole.

That the men in khaki from the central province absorbed the country as though it was only theirs. They took the water, the food, the electricity, the funds; they occupied all the top places – the only places – in the military and the bureaucracy so that their lopsided dominance would never be in danger of being contested, not now, not sixty more years from now.

No one outside of Mir Ali had understood that. It had been as though the others simply did not know it.

But these people, they understood it. The Baloch understood it, that's what his father Inayat had said. The Nepalis too, but Aman Erum had never met any of their number. At Montclair State University there were no Baloch and only one Nepali girl. She wore her hair in a tight ponytail high on her head and, it was said, had grown up in India all her life.

Before he was introduced to phone cards, cheaply bought at all-night corner stores and snow-covered kiosks outside NJ Transit stations, Aman Erum spent the majority of his money left over after food and bills on phone calls home that cost one dollar fifty a minute. Mobile phones were too expensive. Adriana considered calling a relative in California long distance. Aman Erum could not imagine how far away Mir Ali would be on a Sprint or Verizon phone line.

In the early mornings and twilight hours of night, he would collect the change in his pocket – five-cent coins, ten cents, whatever he caught amongst the lint and carefully folded receipts he held on to as evidence of his almost beatific frugality – and unload his palms full of copper and silver into the slot of a payphone, whose mouthpiece was always warm, and dial Mir Ali.

Aman Erum spoke to his family once every two or three weeks, to whoever answered the phone, relaying his news. Three minutes, four maximum. It was all he could afford.

But he always called Samarra once a week, every ten days if the week was too short and the change in his pocket too light. He needed to hear her voice. To have her hear his. What if she forgot him? Aman Erum was still that eleven-year-old boy, waiting by the screen door for the sound of her footsteps on the pebbles outside his house. He sent her letters filled with mementoes of his life in America, colourful bus passes, menus from takeaway restaurants, Amtrak advertisements. He wanted her to see something else, something besides Mir Ali. But she never asked for more, never did anything except drop the souvenirs into a box and forget about them. When Samarra replied to Aman Erum she wrote in Pashto, never in English as he had begun to do. So he called her on the telephone to make up for his absence. As she spoke, Aman Erum would close his eyes and try to memorize her laughter. He said her name, repeatedly, so that she never lost the sound of his voice around it. So that every time someone called her name, she would be able to hear only Aman Erum. He told her everything about his life in New Jersey, about his professors, about his new clothes, about his floor mates and study groups and Adriana and PD and how they helped him fit in and feel at home; he spoke to her about his dreams and his business ideas.

Aman Erum spent his first Eid at Montclair's Masjid Al-Wadud. There were no *imam bargah* nearby, barely a religious inconvenience for Aman Erum, who saw only business opportunities. What else were suburban American cities missing? Where did the faithful buy their prayer caps? How did they import prayer rugs? The Muslims in Aman Erum's dorm prayed on bath mats and wore unembroidered, plain *taqiyeh*. They were too afraid to ask for these things now. 'You see,'

Aman Erum said to Samarra on the telephone, 'I understand vacuums. I understand the psychology of the needy.'

But his conversations with his family were made up largely of his academic pursuits and his economizing, and after hearing a few minutes of what his family had been coping with during his remote continental absence, he put down the phone with a feeling of relief.

Every so often he remembered his gentleman's agreement and would ask his brothers – but never his father, who only spoke to his eldest when he happened to answer the phone, which he did less frequently as he grew more ill and confined himself to his bed – more specific questions about news from Mir Ali. What had happened at the marketplace around the Shirazi slums last Thursday, hadn't there been a tussle between two traders over one of them benefiting from favourable transport routes – had there really been a connection there?

But he knew the real news would never be so casually transmitted over a telephone. Everyone had ears in Mir Ali. Initially he asked so that it would be heard that he had been enquiring.

Aman Erum asked so he would have something to submit – he needed information that would hold his studies on solid ground. Aman Erum probed out of desperation. He wanted to keep himself as far away from Mir Ali as his business studies course would allow.

But as the months drew on he may have begun to overreach. Every once in a while, Aman Erum passed on something good. As the praise and thanks swelled and the months grew colder and darker and his distance from Mir Ali deepened, he no longer withheld what he might previously have counted as sensitive information – strands of stories that, woven together, implicated not just the guilty, but the innocent who protected them.

Aman Erum became reckless. He was too far away to realize

how quickly he had unbraided secrets and how easily those undone by his loose tongue had been condemned. Eventually, when he was back in Mir Ali, it would seem that he no longer cared. But that was later.

Aman Erum sent unprompted reports; he did not bother to wait for Colonel Tarik to place his own calls. He pre-empted him, as he had done with the deal in Islamabad.

If he heard from Zainab or Sikandar that a home had seen its son leave on Monday and that by Wednesday his anxious-looking family had packed all their belongings, stuffing old televisions into cardboard boxes and filling blankets with their kitchen cutlery, tightly knotting the home-made bundles so that the dishes and bowls would not break against each other, Aman Erum connected the dots and placed an urgent phone call to the Colonel's office.

Attack planned, he whispered into the black earpiece. Seems to be imminent, family has fled. Shahzar is expected to target soon. He spoke in dramatic telegram bursts, trying to impress upon the Colonel the gravity of the information he was delivering. In the common room Aman Erum watched police shows on American television where the camaraderie of officials was not broken by fears of informants or counter-information and where men looked out for one another, shielding partners from all manners of distress and instinctively guarding the emotions of a grumpy but entirely well-meaning boss.

It had made him less afraid, more confident and comfortable in his role.

He was doing a service, a long-distance service that only required him to protect the peace.

He had seen his father shout till his voice was hoarse about the cost of life in Mir Ali. How hard it is not to die here, he wheezed, borrowing the phrase from poets past. He had watched Hayat cry at the funerals of his friends, his friends who were his eldest brother's age and who had died fighting in the insurgencies against the army. It was not that Aman Erum did not understand the war. He did. But Aman Erum also thought he understood how power worked and he had no desire to join his father and Hayat in an unwinnable fight.

He dialled the 01192 numbers in the evening, cupping the receiver to his mouth while Adriana flung notebooks at him across the corridors as she slouched back from class. Colonel Tarik had initially sounded surprised to hear his new charge on the phone. Aman Erum thought he was taken aback by his initiative.

'You boys from Mir Ali are not always so cooperative,' the Colonel had said on the first phone call Aman Erum placed spontaneously. 'Welcome, welcome on board.'

Aman Erum had not expected to, but he felt warmed by the Colonel's response. He basked slightly in the approval of the Colonel's voice over the distant line and felt his anxiety over the deal they had struck recede. He was far enough from Mir Ali that he could help the Colonel without being hurtful to anyone. How much more could he possibly know than the glorious Pakistani army? What amount of insider knowledge could he tap into that the generals and majors and cadets around Colonel Tarik didn't already know?

Aman Erum mulled over these thoughts. After the first few phone calls they had seemed less urgent in his mind, more obvious. They, the Colonel and the mysterious American lady who arranged the meeting, had only asked him to let them know what he heard. If he heard something, it can't have been that secret. If Samarra had heard something, it mustn't have been very carefully hidden. Aman Erum did not, not once, stop to wonder how carefully hidden Samarra was.

He was only confirming what they already knew.

Initially he called the Colonel so that they would not revoke his visa, so that they would know he took their deal seriously and that he valued his opportunity to study abroad. Aman Erum, the eldest and most responsible of his brothers, called so that they could not accuse him of reneging on his promise. But then he called to relay news, to speak in code, to be reassured that the Colonel appreciated hearing from him.

'*Grana*, with all this work how are you able to concentrate on your studies?' It had made Aman Erum uncomfortably happy to hear this. For a moment his stomach turned as he stood in the corridor that smelled of sweaty gym socks, and he held the phone silently.

But then the Colonel clicked the phone off the speaker and asked Aman Erum how the weather was and whether he had managed to keep a heater for himself in the room – sometimes the administration did not allow these things but of course sometimes central heating was not sufficient.

And Aman Erum remembered that there was an intimacy they shared.

The Colonel had left him alone; he had given him his freedom because of these pre-emptive calls. Had he not demonstrated his reliability, the Colonel would have been breathing down his neck.

Aman Erum had heard stories like this as he grew up in Mir Ali, stories of collaborators given jobs in the federal capital who became so comfortable with their new lives that they had to be reminded where they came from and who they were.

There were stories of boys, young men, given scholarships and athletic *sifarish* into the national hockey team, who over time forgot that these were favours, and soon found themselves, in all cases, fired. But first they were disgraced.

The man in the capital had to come home. He could not

drive his Korean-made car back to Mir Ali because it had been impounded by the company. He came in a bus, always looking over his shoulder, wearing the clothes he left in, and sat alone in his home while the neighbours whispered. Eventually he stopped leaving his house altogether, no longer attending Friday prayers or local wedding celebrations. He did not walk past the dried-fruit stand, covered by the shade of the Chilgoza pines, to pick up apricots and talk to the aged seller. He did not marry, as his mother had insisted he would as soon as his busy schedule allowed. He was found hanging from his ceiling fan.

But that would never happen to Aman Erum.

Aman Erum couldn't really be called an informer. He was a modern necessity. A function of the days and times we live in. He was the passer-on of news. He could not judge the quality of his news, but he delivered it professionally and this the Colonel respected.

'*Der kha, grana*. Well done. Nice to hear you. Regards to your family from our side. *Akphal khial sata*, take care.'

The line went dead as the Colonel moved on to his papers and newspapers and more important intelligence. Aman Erum put the receiver back on the payphone on the wall. Out of habit he made a point to break the line, as if he were still in Mir Ali – as if these superstitions worked – and then picked it up again, inserted more coins and dialled the number that always followed the Colonel's, the number that wished away the previous call.

'*Salam?*'

She had just woken up, he could hear sleep in her voice.

12

'I'm sorry,' Hayat says. Stepping back he can feel the earth crumble underneath his feet. 'I didn't mean to make you . . . I wasn't . . . I'm not . . .' Hayat loses the words on his lips.

Samarra hasn't lowered her eyes. She stays perfectly still but for a faint movement of her shoulders, which curve slightly as she releases a shallow breath and then straighten as she continues to talk.

'I'm just jumpy.'

He understands. They have been together for two years now. Hayat has seen Samarra on the mornings of serious operations and on the evenings that follow. They have weathered the hours in between for many months now. Not knowing has an effect on most people that makes them nervous or irritable but Samarra is not flustered, not normally. It's the knowing, the afterwards, that takes its toll on her. There were successes and there were captures that she responded to equally, without distinction, then, withdrawing into a space only large enough for her, she vanished for a period. Hayat never asked her where she went or what she did, he only waited until she returned. She never spoke of those solitary retreats either. They had learned each other's codes and adapted themselves to the languages and limitations they required.

'It's big today.' She speaks in empty phrases. She utters only safe sentences on such days, never delivering a hint about the hours ahead. One can track operations in Mir Ali based on Samarra's syntax. She kicks the dirt with her foot, freeing an ankle from underneath her in the process, as she looks at

Hayat. 'It's the biggest we have ever attempted.' He nods. His language on these days is as cryptic as hers.

There is something frail about her this morning, something Hayat hasn't seen previously. It makes her appear unstable, unpredictable.

'Do you know what this will mean?' Samarra is speaking to herself now, sounding jumpier as her words tumble into each other. She talks quickly to get them out. 'It will change the situation. It will be too large an assault. They will have to reconfigure everything. Every security, every informer, every policy will be unmade by it.'

She doesn't have stage fright. She is excited.

'Samarra,' Hayat begins slowly, weighing his words against her timbre, which he can feel building. He won't have another moment; he has already disturbed the protocols Samarra insists upon. 'Are you ready for this?'

She smiles. Hayat looks at her lips as they pull upwards. There had been a different tug, a smaller tilt to her smile when he had first met her.

Mir Ali had always been Hayat's destiny. This he had always known. As a young man enlisting to fight for his home he had been carried by the impermeable optimism of revolutionaries. This was a battle for justice. It was a battle that had claimed multitudes, one in which whole generations of men had been sacrificed, but it was one that was waged towards the light. It would lead, a young Hayat fervently believed, to victory. Because it must. Because Mir Ali would soon be free. It would reclaim its own destiny.

But Mir Ali never did transcend its enemies. Its leaders had broken it down, they had become fanatics. Hayat had trouble recognizing Mir Ali in their eyes. He can no longer see anything in Samarra's. Samarra with the green eyes and the beauty mark trapped inside.

*

Of his brothers, Hayat had listened to his father's stories with the deepest interest. He sat with Inayat while he worked, and concentrated on the tales Inayat traded with his friends over tea, boiled in an aged samovar and spiced with poppy seeds and cardamom in the Afghan style.

Inayat told Hayat fables as they walked in the evenings, preparing to head home for dinner. Hayat always went straight to his father's carpet store after school, and later, when the family's fortunes had changed, to his workshop.

Leaning slightly on his son, his elbow bent into a triangle over Hayat's shoulder, Inayat spoke to his son in parables.

He told him the story of a king so generous he had fed the fish in his kingdom's river with grains and pressed silver coins into the palms of beggars until one day he discovered that he had been edged out of his own kingdom. The king wandered through the forests until he had resigned himself to the life of a fakir and found himself at the entrance of another man's kingdom. Approaching the new king, whose people knew him as an avaricious and cruel monarch, the once-royal fakir asked for his help, for a meal and a place to rest his aching soles.

The greedy king agreed, promising to feed and keep the wanderer in luxury for several months after which a service would be asked of him. I am at your mercy, the fakir said, ever so grateful. Some months later, maybe six, maybe seven, the king collected the fakir, well fed and rested from his travels, and took him to be sewn into the hide of a slaughtered ox. When he questioned his lord why he must be hidden in the leather of the ox's belly, the king reminded the fakir of his generosity and told him this was the deal they had agreed upon.

The fakir submitted himself and, once wrapped, he was carried away by an enormous creature with large claws and long, bristly feathers to the summit of a mountain. You will come down with my instructions, the king bellowed from below, once you have thrown me all the diamonds lying around the mountain.

The fakir obeyed. He nicked his fingers on the uncut stones as he sent them down to the insatiable king, circling the expanse of the mountain while his feet bled. When he had emptied the soil of its jewels he asked the king if he could come back down. As he was pleading to be told how to descend, the king called up one more question to the fakir.

Do you see bones now, uncovered by the gems, on the mountaintop?

The fakir lowered his eyes and saw that the ground was littered with human skeletons. There are many, he shouted back. I see them. But the greedy king had gone, carrying off his diamonds.

Inayat always stopped, he always stopped at this point and removed his arm from his son, who grew taller and taller, making the use of his shoulder as a crutch uncomfortable, and looked at him. 'Do you see, Hayat *jan*,' he said, using his son's name in duplicate, 'do you see, Hayat, my life, what they have done to us?' My soul, my life.

Inayat did not finish the tale, did not end the folk legend with the rest of the story, which saw the fakir throw himself off the mountain into the river below it, where he was saved by the very fish that had fattened themselves on his alms of grain. Inayat did not end the legend with its message of revenge.

The fakir returned to the insatiable king, who was shocked to see him alive. The fakir told the king he would show him the easy way down the mountain if he would sew himself into an ox's hide and be placed, as he had placed so many others, at the mountain's peak. Greedily, the king agreed. He couldn't resist – the diamonds would then be within his direct reach. Once at the summit, the king danced among the diamonds and was hurriedly gathering as many as he could into his hands when he caught sight of the fakir walking away from their deal.

Where are you going? he yelled to the wanderer. You have to show me how to return.

You love nothing more than those diamonds, the fakir replied, now live among them. And he walked back to the kingdom, where he was placed on the throne vacated by the insatiable king.

This part Inayat omitted.

All children knew the tale; it was a popular Pashtun story passed down to remind the young of the consequences of desire and greed. But Inayat never recited the tale's end. He stopped on the street, the dust swirling round his sandalled feet in the evening breeze, and spoke to his son.

'You see, you see what they have taken from us?'

Inayat spoke the moral of the story to the one son who knew how precious the summit of Mir Ali was.

As Inayat felt himself closer and closer to death, he repeated to Zainab the value of the home they had built together and circled numbers and digits into the air so that she would know, after a lifetime together, what it was that he was leaving to her and their sons. As the night blackened over Mir Ali, lighting the sky with nothing save for a constellation of stars so faint you would think they shone over another city, casting a glow on Mir Ali only out of pity, Inayat bade Aman Erum farewell and, suppressing the disappointment in his voice, wished him success in his endeavours. Inayat said he knew his son would do well in business. To Sikandar and Mina he had no final consolations to offer. He had had nothing to say to them for some time. Their grief made him dumb and in his own passing he did not want to aggrieve them further. Inayat saw Hayat last.

He had saved him, his youngest boy, so that his lips would close upon the words he murmured into his son's ear.

'Come to my grave and tell me Mir Ali is free. Whisper it to me, even when I'm gone.'

10:27

13

Refugees of the drone war in neighbouring Waziristan towns and villages escaped the fighting in their homes by living like ghosts on the outskirts of Mir Ali. They were easily recruited by the militia who lived in the forests and hills, waging their own bloody war against the state. Truth be told, they were the easiest. They were easily recruited because they had nothing left to defend.

The militants, as they were called by journalists and foreigners, were fighting the excesses of a corrupt, godless nation. They did not flinch from violence. They beheaded soldiers and kidnapped brigadiers. We are close, they said, we are so close you can feel our breath upon your neck.

But they were not welcomed, not well received, not initially at least, by the local population. The militants expected to be welcomed like heroes, they thought themselves heroes. And why not? Look at the battles they pitched against the state. The state that everyone hated, that burned everyone's skin. But they were not heroes.

They received money wherever it presented itself. They confiscated bootleg alcohol, condemning to death the Sikh and Christian minorities that survived on the trade, and sold the rusted cans and glass bottles to enlarge their own caches. They took money from mosques that raised pennies from congregants, and they received foreigners from bright green countries that dutifully supported their cause to the tune of millions.

There was little by way of violence and corruption that separated them from their enemies. They heard what those in the cities said about them – that they paid men to detonate bands of dynamite strapped to their unwilling chests for cash amounts of forty thousand, thirty thousand, twenty, ten.

It was not true per se. The militants did not give the soon-to-be-deceased man a briefcase of money – money that he could never spend should he choose to accept the mission. But they did support the man's family and his children for what was deemed to be a suitable amount of compensatory time.

There was one distinguishing feature between the militants and the men they fought: they were true believers. These men were imbued with the message of the righteous and led by the certainty of their faith. They were an army devoted to the *sunna*. They lived and fought according to the sayings and scriptures of God. Their God was mightier than the fifth-largest army in the world. A nation of one hundred and eighty million people was no match for their God. They saw themselves as holy warriors, they defended a book they had never learned to read in a language they could not speak.

There was nothing godless about the men on the margins of Mir Ali.

A shot is fired. The sound rings mercilessly in Sikandar's ears. He slams his foot on the brakes of the van. His body is thrown back against his seat. He can't tell if the shot was fired at the vehicle, at them – at him or Mina – or as a warning, directed into the sky. Sikandar pats his chest, looks at his legs. He can hear the crunch of the grit beneath the van's wheels.

He's fine. He's not hurt. Mina, also hurled back against her seat, has a look of intense anger on her face. He scans her legs, her arms, until he's certain she hasn't been hit.

Sikandar feels an instant relief: it wasn't them. It was a mistake. It was a stray bullet. The firing must have been directed elsewhere. He is putting his hand on the door when Mina grabs his wrist.

'Don't,' she whispers, her carefully stored anger on the verge of escaping her.

Sikandar turns his face away from the door and looks at Mina. 'I have to check if the van was damaged.' He assures her: 'I'm not leaving you.'

As the muscles in his hand flex to grip the door handle, Sikandar hears a whistling crack. He turns to see his window being smashed inwards and feels the butt of an assault rifle ram into his jaw.

Mina howls, Sikandar hears her – it registers as a loud, desperate wail. For a moment, he can't see. There is a buzzing behind his left eye that he hears somewhere in his body; he can't tell if it's his ears that clock the sound or some deep, frightened part of his brain.

His heartbeat races and then slows as he opens his eyes, straining to see, as if he could, what has just happened to him. His legs feel cold; he doesn't dare look down to his feet. Sikandar runs his tongue over the inside of his cheek and across his gums; he can taste the iron in his bloodied mouth. His neck hurts as he tries to move his head to face his attackers. There is a pulse that reacts, throbbing with every fraction of a millimetre that his body moves.

He sees three men, tall rangy-looking men in their late twenties wearing *shalwar kameez* frayed at the collars and cuffs. Woollen shawls wrapped round their bodies are held down by Kalashnikovs and assault rifles strung over their shoulders, layered upon each other like loose strands of jewellery.

The man standing by Mina's window points his gun at her face while casting his eyes away from her. He wears a light-blue turban on his head, tied at the side with the rest of the cloth falling across his shoulder.

A second man is positioning himself at the front of the van, holding his Kalashnikov as though it were a baby, cradling it in his arms and directing his eyes, under heavy brows, at the scene before him. He looks at his two comrades as though he does not trust them entirely, as though he's here to watch them as much as the two strangers in the Hasan Faraz Government Hospital supply van.

The man by Sikandar's window is gaunt, his beard thin and ragged, and though his skin is sallow, pointing to malnutrition and even exhaustion, his eyes gleam in the early morning light. His high cheekbones are painted in a gentle sunburn that brings colour to his face. The skin on his nose is lightly peeling.

'What are you doing here?' he barks, roughly slamming the butt of his weapon into Sikandar's shoulder. 'Who allowed you to come into this area?'

Sikandar is quiet.

He's heard around the hospital that the militants seek out doctors. One oncologist had been roused out of bed early in the morning by the sound of a car outside his front door. Dressed in his pyjamas and a pair of slippers he opened the door to find a grizzled man stepping out of a four-by-four truck filled with men. The man entered the oncologist's home, seated himself in his drawing room and presented him with a stack of yellow chits. Whenever you receive one of these chits, he instructed the oncologist, you are to do whatever is necessary to help. Any man that carries one of these chits comes from my camp, you understand? Your failure to provide immediate medical care to him will be an insult that we will not tolerate. The oncologist was told his services would be free, discreet and constant. They knew where he worked, the names of his secretary and assistant at the hospital. If he did not do as he had been asked, it would be said that he was a collaborator with the state and its army. Everybody knew what happened to unlucky collaborators in Mir Ali.

'*Wia!*' Speak! The rebel at the window screams, and holding his Kalashnikov with both hands he raises it and brings it down over Sikandar's skull. Sikandar feels the dull thud of the butt at the back of his throat. He is unused to violence. Even with two brothers, Sikandar never experienced anything rougher than a bit of play fighting.

He has never been this deep into the forest; he has no idea what chance of survival he has. He does not want to die.

'*Saib*, sir,' Sikandar begins, speaking softly, lowering his shoulders and putting his hands above the steering wheel so all three men can see that he is unarmed, 'I'm just a driver.'

Mina doesn't breathe.

The light rise and fall of her chest stops. She stares at her husband.

The man near Mina's window speaks next. Mina had rolled down the window upon his instruction, but Sikandar can't remember when. He can smell the pines – their scent travels with the rain.

'Who is she?' The man still does not look at her.

'A doctor. I work at the government hospital.' Sikandar lowers his eyes now too. His heart beats fast, faster than he knows to be medically sound. The blood in his mouth and the drumming in his chest compete for panic. He doesn't know which to focus on, which to be more concerned about. He remembers Aman Erum's white and red business card with its website and email addresses and numerous mobile phone numbers. Sikandar had forgotten to pass it on to his colleague, the doctor with the Islamabad Corolla. It is still in his wallet.

'You two are alone?'

'Eid, *saib*, there was no one else to accompany the lady. I was the only driver on duty.' Sikandar leans towards the window.

He can't look at Mina. He feels her breathing slow and her temper return, rising out of her momentary confusion and fear. It bears down upon his back. He feels it.

The gaunt rebel, who wears the tired appearance of a man in charge, takes stock of Sikandar's neatly groomed salt and pepper beard. His eyes dart over Sikandar's clean, freshly starched *shalwar kameez*, the knees of which have never been darned, the pockets fine and tailored with a crisp square pattern on his heart. He looks at his two comrades. The three of them register each other's disbelief. They saw how Mina's face fell as the man spoke, how she followed every turn of his words, how she opened her mouth to speak several times, then didn't utter a sound, letting her driver talk for her.

Mina holds her tightly packed bag to her chest and wishes she had kept her mobile phone on her lap. She raises herself upright after hesitating briefly, straightening her posture, and then sinking back into the seat before commanding herself to return to the earlier, slightly more authoritative stance. She speaks to the man at her window, slowly. She is careful not to let the turbulence she feels towards Sikandar infect her words.

'*Ror*, brother, I am a doctor. I have been called to deliver a child in this area, a child whose life is in danger of being over before it has begun.' She examines the man above his Kalashnikov, weathered from decades past, and places her palm on the window that separates them. 'Please let us go,' she pleads, careful to keep her voice from sounding desperate. But she already sounds too urgent.

The rebel with the light-blue turban ignores her. He still refuses to meet Mina's eyes. He walks over to Sikandar's side of the van and speaks into the commander's ear.

14

They have to wait. There are no formal rules or codes to this sort of a day, but it is understood by all the people involved that they had better be comfortable with waiting. There are the inevitable delays – traffic, a lookout warning against exposure, a faulty mechanism that threatens to diminish the quality of the explosive attack. There are human errors that result in time spent counting flies or kicking dirt around and then there's just timing.

Nasir has returned home to share an hour with his family that they will notice nothing special about.

They will remember later that he left early in the morning, before drinking his milky tea with the rest of the family. They will recall that it was after only a short absence that Nasir returned home and sat in the living room, trying, it will seem, to bring no one's attention towards his presence but at the same time nestling himself among them.

The men do not often go home, not because their families would dissuade them. To have a son die for Mir Ali would secure a family's honour for generations, worth the eternities of harassment and suspicion from the state that would automatically ensue. They don't go home because they cannot tell their families; they cannot risk word travelling. They cannot compromise the silence of the operation with new ears and mouths.

So they play cards with friends or sit in a *chaikhana* and sip drinks that have no flavour in the face of what lies ahead of them. The goat's milk loses its sour undertaste, the burned sugar of tea cooked in a saucepan tastes heavily of syrup and is vaguely medicinal, and green tea is reduced to water and only the faintest hint of aniseed.

They have to wait. Hayat knew this morning would be interminable. Having this time with her won't make the waiting, or what is to come once the waiting is done, easier, but it's time with Samarra all the same. He is guiltily appreciative of that.

She wants to break out of code; she is desperate to talk in full sentences.

'Why did you ask me if I'm ready?' She winds and unwinds her hair into a bun, holding it in with a pencil. 'Do you think I'm not prepared?'

Hayat watches Samarra's hands weave through her hair as he sits on the dirt ground in front of her. They had unmade her, those beasts. They smelled the weak and swooped down only upon those whose resistance to them would be futile. But she had fought. Initially no one had understood how they found her, how they knew that she was the one to attack.

She had just joined the university and had been working with the men for only a short while, transporting papers and moving radio equipment. She hadn't told a soul about her second, clandestine, non-house-girl life.

Almost no one.

But, even then, she hadn't betrayed a man.

When they released her she did not speak of what they did or what hands had been laid on her.

But she fought back. She fought back to prove her innocence, hers and Ghazan Afridi's. She fought on behalf of her missing father. Samarra remembered his promise of the coming years. She fought to believe it was still possible. She fought to establish her unbroken credibility with the men who looked nervous about asking her to continue with her work. She fought to erase from her life the man with the medals on his chest and the rose-gold wedding ring on his finger.

She fought so hard that she had started to become like them.

'I've been waiting years for this. If anyone can lead this operation, it's me. You know that. What did you mean? Did the others say they felt insecure?'

'No, it's not that.' Hayat edges slightly closer to her, close enough to smell the jasmines on her wrist. 'Samarra, this is bigger than anything else. We need time. We need time to think about what will happen afterwards; we need time to protect our people, our homes; we need time to consider what the blowback will be.'

Her smile, the curious one, returns.

Today, just before the wail of the muezzin calls the scattered men of Mir Ali to Friday prayers, there is to be a ceremony. It has been timed for today, for the Friday that falls on Eid, because it is a celebratory occasion.

The Chief Minister of the frontier state is coming all the way from his whitewashed bungalow in the capital to preside over the induction of four hundred of Mir Ali's finest into the national army.

There had been an unofficial block against men from these parts joining the armed services for decades. They were separatists, untrustworthy, not deemed fit for active duty in any of the three branches – not the navy, not the army and certainly not the air force. The most gentlemanly of the three barely took anyone from outside the central province.

The unofficial block was politically denied. Anyone who wished to serve their country was welcome to submit an application, then all they had to do was pass the tests. But the army always suspected that anyone applying from Mir Ali or its environs was attempting not to assimilate, but to infiltrate and so they closed the door to them.

When periods of insurgency raged, there was a more official ban. They were not welcomed in any state institutions. Not the National Bank, not the Ministry of Foreign Affairs.

But, recently, the state had smartened up. It was never going to win a long-drawn-out war against men who had nothing to lose. It was never going to succeed in condemning these men already relegated to the fringes. They belonged nowhere. They had nothing of their own. But if the state could draw them in, connect them to the centre they fought so furiously against, if it could co-opt them, it would neutralize their disruptions. Soft benefits were introduced first. There were visa lotteries to study and migrate abroad, but that was too obvious, too clear that the state was trying, with the help of its foreign friends, to repatriate Mir Ali's young. Those who had initially lined up to receive emigration papers to Britain and study visas to America were shamed into tearing up their applications. The humiliation remained, however. It clung to them. Only those with ambition larger than shame, with individual desires that were stronger than the struggles of the collective, went ahead and left anyway. Most of those men never returned. They cut their ties with Mir Ali. But Aman Erum left with his head held high; no one would suspect his sympathies. He was Inayat's son. He was Hayat's brother. He was Samarra Afridi's.

Next, the state opened up small ministries, the most corrupt ones where no effort was expended and no work ever accomplished – the Ministry of Health, largely – for junior civil servant positions. When the press beat their drums about the miserly amount of the budget given to the federal ministry of health and education they would now have to consider how the state was also generously accommodating these tribals, these would-be warriors. They were invited to big cities to administer government dispensaries or deal with the foreign sales of disinfectants that could not be consumed as alcohol. Petty work, doctors need not apply.

But it wasn't enough. They would never be placated in these ways alone. They had to be brought into the belly of the beast.

The pilot project was to start with four hundred in the army. They would be sent to serve in various parts of the country. They would become a part of the machinery they assumed worked only against their people. In time they would see that it worked against everyone. They road-blocked Quetta. Stood under bridges in Karachi, stopping cars driving to the airport or heading out of the city at random. They guarded ministries in Peshawar.

They were no one's oppressors. They were everyone's oppressors.

The Chief Minister had been crowing about this grand new gesture, this step of greater inclusion, for weeks now. The recruits had been carefully secreted away at the army base where they had been receiving their initial training.

No mention was made of their names, how they were selected, or how they were even approached (no one in the town could recall a recruitment drive). After a five-week initiation course, Mir Ali's four hundred would be formally inducted into the armed forces. The Khakis would make sure not to have any of their new recruits photographed at the function – there would be no faces visible in the photographs released to the press. No identifying features of the military trainers and absolutely no glances of the freshly trained men.

The Chief Minister would get all the attention.

The Chief Minister held what seemed like weekly press conferences about his upcoming trip. 'This is a historic undertaking,' he said when he announced his programme to visit Mir Ali.

Whether the minister was opening a tyre factory or meeting the families of jailed opponents, he wore a starched black *sherwani*, the collar thick and stiff round his neck. Men's sandals made from distressed leather for the day and, for the evening, black patent shoes shined severely by his footman. His hair was dyed boot-polish black to match the hair on his arms, which crept up the back of his hands and over his knuckles.

He was a political appointee; he had never won an election in his life.

'The only thing,' the Chief Minister promised the media last week, 'that will once and for all time end militancy in Mir Ali is development and reconciliation.'

Had he ever been to Mir Ali before, journalists asked the Chief Minister, shoving microphones in his face.

No, no, he hadn't. But he had met many people who had been to Mir Ali, who assured him that the people there wanted nothing more than to be a part of Pakistan's future. 'They do not want violence, they want reconciliation. They are ready to reconcile with us. We must extend to them a hand of friendship.' With this he proffered a hirsute hand to the crowd of hacks and smiled widely at the assembled cameramen.

He promised, though it was not his remit to do so, that by next year there would be a thousand new recruits inducted from Mir Ali. The year after that, double.

'If we were not serious about this reconciliation process we would not be launching this five-year plan. By the end of which, we will have many thousands of men from Mir Ali, and women possibly, serving in the national army.' The military had no such plans, no such five-year promises, but the minister drew great applause from the suggestion that they might.

He was coming to Mir Ali to spend Eid with his 'most important family – the people' and to launch this great new collaboration. There was enthusiasm about his optimism. It was a bright and bold new step.

Samarra smiles. Hayat watches her, she looks calm suddenly. She stops fidgeting with her hair – now loose and combed through by her hand as she plays with her pencil, slipping it in and out of her fingers like running water. Hayat looks at her lips. He doesn't realize he is holding his breath. Samarra speaks in a voice that breaks through her smile as she responds to Hayat.

'You're right, this is the biggest thing we'll ever do. We don't need more time. It's today, Hayat. We're ready.'

Hayat thinks he sees Samarra restraining a laugh.

'We're going to kill the Chief Minister.'

15

'*Salam, zama khog.*'

Aman Erum always began the phone calls like that, calling her 'my dear'. He liked that she woke up instantly with the sound of the phone ringing but that she took no trouble to conceal her sleepy voice.

'It's you.'

She always sounded surprised.

'I've been in class all day – couldn't call you late last night but didn't want to miss you before you started your day.'

'*Sa masla na dey.*' No problem. Samarra yawned between the gaps in the words.

He could hear her getting up and imagined her brushing her long hair. While she moved loudly around her room, holding the phone between her ear and her shoulder, Aman Erum told her about his professors, men who asked to be called by their first names, and new clubs he had joined at the start of term – he was most excited by the International Business Society. He thought he might even run to be a part of its council.

She made polite noises and then –

'When are you coming back?'

'Coming back?'

'Home. When are you going to come back home?'

'Well, I can't come between semesters; you know that. It costs me so much to be here. Until I can rent a place that's cheaper, just my housing is the price of two return tickets.'

'No, I mean, when will this all be over, when will you have the degree that you left everything for?'

She meant herself. Samarra remembered the light-blue pick-up truck and the jerrycan of petrol between Aman Erum's knees the summer he left her in Mir Ali. The adults were abandoning Ghazan Afridi and Aman Erum comforted Samarra while packing for Chitral. Years, he had said to her. Maybe years. When Samarra walked away that day, when she left in the middle of a conversation she wished he had never started, Aman Erum didn't follow her. Samarra stood outside the gate protecting the house on Sher Hakimullah road for a minute, waiting for him, giving him time to jump off the pick-up truck and trace her steps. She waited for him to come and apologize to her. To bow his head and say that it would not be years. Not years. He hadn't meant years at all.

And then she heard the sound of the light-blue pick-up's engine starting.

Aman Erum was getting tired of this refrain. She always asked when he was coming back home. She never asked when he would return to her, it was always Mir Ali.

'Samarra, *zama khog*, it's going to take some time.'

'I know the business degrees there take three years. Why does yours take longer?'

Aman Erum had not told her that, in fact, it didn't take longer. He would be done in three years but was planning on working once he was done, on renting a small apartment and making a new life for himself here. He had told her, obliquely, of his plans to settle away from Mir Ali. She had told him, adamantly, that she would not go. Their conversations were beginning to become wearisome.

'Tell me, what are you doing today?'

She was silent. He allowed her a costly minute of sulking.

'What have you planned for the day?' he repeated, as if saying it for the first time.

The sound of movement started again. She put down the phone to get dressed, picking it up again mid-answer.

'. . . to Zain ul Abeddin's mother. She's in such a state.'

'What happened to Zain ul Abeddin?'

Aman Erum straightened his back against the wall. He hadn't heard anything about their classmate. He was a short, rambunctious art student. Always covered in specks of paint and smelling of turpentine.

Apart from Samarra, Aman Erum hadn't really had friends in Mir Ali. The people who shook his hand as they passed by him in the library or who stopped to chat as they held cigarettes over steaming glass cups of *elaichi* green tea, were Samarra's friends, not his. He knew people, but he interacted with the world through her.

In truth, he had never really bothered to reach out to new people, not till now. Here in America there were long tables full of eager faces he felt inclined towards. Inspired by Panthea's nickname – her name turned out to be completely unpronounceable to American tongues, sounding almost rude when they tried – Aman Erum had also started to go by his initials. AE. Aman Erum had never met so many people just like himself.

Here, they thought of nothing but growth. Aman Erum had felt alone in Mir Ali. There had been so few like him; no one who wanted to break free of duty, no one dedicated to the future.

Those young men at the Shah Sawar net café weren't like him. They were voyeurs, unambitious peeping toms. They just wanted to have a sniff of what lay outside Mir Ali, nothing more. They might bother Rustam to fill out a form and write an application for them but they didn't have the drive that it

took to get out. They were constantly delayed by their obliga-
tions. But here in New Jersey Aman Erum met immigrants
with dreams as expansive as his own.

'No, nothing,' Samarra said quietly. 'He's fine.'

'What, then? I thought you said something happened to
him?'

'No, he's just away for some time.'

'But what happened that he had to travel?'

Aman Erum asked this too eagerly.

'Why are you so interested? You barely even knew him.'

At home Aman Erum inherited friends, from his brothers,
drawn from the children of his parents' acquaintances, from
Samarra, who knew and was known by everybody, and as such
they were floaters of friends. He saw them when he had no
choice but to be seen by them. They came with other people's
timetables and visiting hours.

But here, Aman Erum sat in the common room with Adriana and PD, eating salty food and watching detective shows
that ran on television from five in the evening till seven thirty.
When one channel moved to cover the news they would simply switch channels and find a new episode of their show
mid-broadcast. When someone correctly guessed the guilty
party on the show, usually Adriana, Aman Erum and PD
slapped their friend's hand in the air and cheered.

Here he had friends. Aman Erum felt safe in the common
rooms and dining halls and he made his telephone calls freely
now, not waiting till the rest of the floor had retired to sleep or
gone out for the evening.

'I knew him.'

Aman Erum felt his throat clench. Unlike his mother, who
traded in such gossip freely, Samarra saw it as a needless dis-
traction. Neither of his brothers had mentioned Zain ul
Abeddin's disappearance. Sikandar had said only that some

weeks back there had been a car laden with explosives found near the university. The key had been in the ignition, the driver had left a burning cigarette in the ashtray. He had only just got out of the car when the military police, seeing the car and not recognizing the Charsadda licence plates, approached the vehicle. No one had mentioned to Aman Erum that one of his own classmates had been behind the wheel of the ticking time-bomb car. Had Zain ul Abeddin been behind the wheel? Aman Erum caught himself. It almost didn't matter. He had a name.

'Don't change the subject, Aman Erum. Will you be home next year?'

He demurred. He hoped so, but it was a very tough situation, having to study and work in the admissions office as well as stay in touch with his family. He was doing his best under the difficult circumstances he was placed in. Could he call her next week for a longer talk? He just remembered he had to turn in a recitation assignment before the day's end, five hundred words on managerial economics.

Samarra wished Aman Erum luck in catching the recitation deadline – she learned all these words with him and adopted them quickly as her own so that they wouldn't sound as foreign on her tongue as they did when she heard them slip off his. 'I'm thinking of you,' she said shyly in English, even more quietly than she had spoken Zain ul Abeddin's name, copying the words as she had heard them on a television drama filmed in Karachi.

But Aman Erum didn't hear her. He had replaced the receiver, then counted a second before picking it up again and punching in the twelve-digit number from his frayed phone card.

10:45

16

When they found Samarra, when the Colonel traced the very bountiful information back to the lady with the silver bracelet on her wrist who attended university classes through the winter and Eid and summer holidays, spending two hours at the library when the main buildings were closed, they wasted very little time.

Aman Erum's information had been too direct, too good. It had to have been coming from the source. He handed over too many half names which led them to many otherwise hidden men. They knew – they were in the business of knowing such things about their informants – that Aman Erum was not involved himself. But what terrorist in this backwoods North Waziristan village could be so stupid as to hand out cadre details – names, not only of those who had recently vanished on medical business or urgent family matters, but also those of recently anguished mothers who had no visible reason to be distressed. Thanks to Aman Erum the Khakis were in possession of small findings, two-hour windows' worth of leads, noticeably more precise than the empty threats and useless tips normally placed before their telephone operators and fax machines.

Aman Erum had got so good at delivering these timely titbits that they almost reconsidered having the girl picked up. The supply would stop, the thread would be cut. But in the end it was too tempting not to squeeze her.

Aman Erum stands on a crowded street corner. He throws a glance over his shoulder, rubbing his hands to ward off the cold. He has been walking around Mir Ali for an hour now, circling the area around Pir Roshan road and doubling over his tracks. The Colonel never leaves Bismillah Travels when he does. He manages to be in Mir Ali and to be absent from it, to be unseen and unheard of in the very place his forces control. No one even knows the man's name here.

When old men in markets and young rebels in underground cells speak of the military, they spit out the name of the Chief of Army Staff, ejecting his name forcefully so that they will not have to linger on its letters. They mutter invectives against famous generals who have been presidents or those who soon will be. But they don't know the names of the corps commanders or those who serve as unlisted intelligence officials.

Aman Erum looks back once more to confirm he is alone.

Even he doesn't know what Colonel Tarik Irshad does in the armed forces. He has never seen a designation on a business card, never heard his name pelted like a stone in protests or at press club meets. But he is more powerful than those portly, English-accented generals whose names are spoken on local TV channels. This Aman Erum is sure of.

How they took Samarra he has never found out.

The Colonel never spoke to Aman Erum about what happened, and Aman Erum never dared to ask. She has refused to see him since his return to Mir Ali. She won't answer his calls or return his letters. Aman Erum stood on Samarra's doorstep one afternoon and waited for her to come out. After two hours had passed with no movement, he knocked, softly. Her mother, Malalai, opened the door only enough to see who was outside. When she saw Aman Erum, just the same as he had been when he left, Malalai opened the door wide and took him into her arms. 'Aman Erum, *bachaya*, when did you return?' She was smiling, happy to see him. Samarra hadn't told her anything about him, about them. About what had happened.

She had no idea that Aman Erum was back even though for a month he had called every day and pushed letters under the door. How had Samarra kept all that from her mother? He hadn't felt brave enough to contact Samarra before then. He thought he was making up for his long absence, reaching out to her now that enough time had passed. But her mother didn't even know he was back.

'Is Samarra here, Malalai *taroray*?' Aman Erum asked nervously, after ten minutes of standing at the door. 'I'd really like to see her.'

Malalai nodded excitedly, 'Of course, of course.' She looked behind her. Samarra's bedroom was shut. Malalai shuffled towards her daughter's room and leaned on the door. 'Samarra, Samarra.' Aman Erum could hear her moving; his heart beat with the certainty that he could hear her footsteps. Slowly, the door opened and Samarra's mother smiled and clapped her hands with the good news. 'Aman Erum is here, he's back.' She spoke too soon. Samarra heard her mother only once she'd stepped outside her room. She stood there for a second. She saw him standing at the front door. Aman Erum saw that she saw him. He opened his mouth to speak, to say something, anything. *Salam*, maybe, like he had once done as a young boy, but before he could think of the words, Samarra looked back at her mother. 'Tell him I'm not here,' she said calmly, then she shut her bedroom door and turned the lock.

All Aman Erum hears of her now is through Hayat. He hears of Samarra only through his brother. His Samarra. Samarra Afridi with the messy hair and the footsteps, the sound of which, pounding on the pebbles outside his house, he never forgot. He could not bear to think of the pain he had caused her. In the small of the night, as Aman Erum lay in bed thinking about Samarra, he comforted himself with the hope that one day he might convince her to speak to him again, to see him, and to forgive what he had done. He would write her letters, more letters, and he would speak to her mother. He would sit by his screen door and wait. Aman Erum took solace, for a time, in the unsaid. But he knew, in those late hours before twilight, that he had lost her for ever. And, at that moment, he hated Mir Ali for what they had both become.

She had been walking home in the afternoon – no later than four, just as the sun had begun to descend over the pass. It had a curious effect, burning the gravel and the dirt floors of Mir Ali's foundation and warming the ground before the cool evening air appeared to distort the temperature.

Two cars stopped, one in front of her and one alongside her on the road. They were unmarked, but they did not bother to tint their windows. There was no need for such flourishes. There was no one the state needed to hide from, not here in Mir Ali. The soldiers were not the same as the ones who manned the checkpoints and interrogated drivers on the particulars of their identity cards. They were not the same, certainly not the same, as the men stationed at roundabouts and mosques ahead of important and inflammatory holidays. They were better. They were stronger. They swooped in on Samarra with the delicacy of fireflies.

Samarra felt their breath behind her ears before she heard their footsteps. Their boots had not disturbed the sand on which she stood. Their soles had barely stirred the earth.

The car doors were kept open. Before she understood what was happening, she had been lifted off the ground. The sound of the engine starting vibrated against her cheeks. Her hands had been bound and a filthy rag, smelling of sweat and of diesel, had been placed over her like a shroud.

Samarra didn't scream. She didn't utter a word.

'*Zache zoo*,' a voice behind her said.

Another voice laughed. 'What's the rush?'

'I want to get a look at her before the boss does.'

Another voice. It was closer than the first.

They were speaking in Pashto. They weren't locals – she could hear their stumbling. They tripped over the language, stubbing their feet against it as they talked. They spoke her language so she'd understand them. They weren't locals. But they pretended they were. They thought they could make her believe that everyone was a collaborator, that everyone around her was theirs.

The drive wasn't long – they had houses and offices everywhere – and as the car shut off its engine, Samarra was pushed out of the car, and pulled by her clothes to a standing position and into a warm room. The chair she was placed on was foldable, cold, and Samarra attempted to stretch her fingers across her seat to see how much space she occupied. She had no sense of whether she was alone or not. The gunnysack that covered her face and torso stank of others, of people before her. It confused her. Was that her sweat that smelled so rancid? Was it her breath that clung to the fabric? She couldn't tell.

'*Zama lur, zama lur,* what sort of young woman finds herself in a police cell?'

Samarra could not see the face of the man who called her his daughter. She only felt him move round her chair, circling her slowly before taking a seat across from her. As he sat down she felt the air round her compress. There was no table between them.

'What sort of woman, tell me, knows things that she shouldn't? Matters that don't concern her. How do you know those things, *zama lur*?'

Samarra shook her head. She shook the fabric from side to

163

side but its heavy knit didn't provide space for her eyes to see through. She felt his knees rub against hers.

'Is that bothering you? I will have it removed at once.'

He reached over and tugged at the cloth, not too hard, not so much that her body jerked forward, but not so gently either.

'It has your scent on it now.'

He touched it to his nose. He hadn't taken his eyes off her.

Bags under his eyes, darkly lined as if the sun had shaded in his skin, drew down his thin face. Smatterings of sunspots gave the impression of middle age. Benign, a soon-to-be-retired military man. She could not tell his rank, but he wore medals upon his breast.

'Why am I here?'

She had no other words.

'My dear, you are here because you have betrayed your people. What does a beautiful young girl like you gain from attacking our country?'

'It is not my country.'

Samarra flinched as she said the words, she flinched as she heard them spoken aloud, and she braced herself to be hit. She had heard enough stories to know the tempo of these meetings. Samarra knew from cousins and comrades and classmates how dangerous uncensored, impolite voices had become in Mir Ali.

But he laughed. He leaned forward and laughed at her.

'Do you think yourself greater than it? Do you think that this nation will fold up simply because two hundred border peasants wish to belong to Afghanistan?' He spat the words at her. 'It is not your country, you are right. You are not fit for it.'

Samarra lowered her eyes. And just as her lids closed, the split second in which her lashes locked and became tangled with each other, the instant her eyes closed in a blink, she was blown off her chair. She would never hear out of her right ear again.

As Samarra lay on the floor, twisted onto her side with her

hands still bound behind her back, the man stood up. He unbuckled or unbuttoned something. She heard a click and waited, holding her breath. The sound was followed by a small thud, something being placed on one of the folding chairs, and then the sound of him walking towards her. He stood on her hair in his standard-issue ox-blood boots. From where she lay, Samarra could see how his leather boots shone against the grime of the floor.

'What do you think we do with women like you?'

Samarra could not see his face; she could only feel the pull of his boots. Her scalp throbbed as he squatted down to speak to her.

'What do you think happens to *baghi* like you?'

'I'm not a rebel.'

She closed her eyes in preparation for the second strike. How had they found her? Who had been careless enough to expose her to these men? Everyone knew what they did with women like her. Not so many years before, they'd read in the papers of women doctors and secretaries raped in Balochistan's Sui gas fields because they had spoken too loudly of the state's pilfering. A consultant who had been hired from her southern city to come and put together a report on the gas fields was raped and beaten in her official bungalow, the home let to her by the government, and left for dead one November.

But she survived and accused one of her superiors of ordering and orchestrating the twenty-three hours of abuse that ought to have killed her questioning spirit. She was later admitted to an asylum for the infirm and insane.

Her rapists never made it to court.

Who could have been treacherous enough to name her when they knew – in Mir Ali everybody knew – what these men did to women like her? She could not think of a single soul.

'How do you know the things you do?'

He cocked his head to the side, looking at Samarra. Her cheek was pressed against the floor and her skin was red and torn from his hand.

He stood up again and dug one of his ox-blood boots into her face. She bit her tongue involuntarily. Her jaw clicked against his heel.

'How do you know who is no longer enrolled in university before the registrar does? How do you know which families have closed their shops to retire to the mountains before they pass our checkpoints?'

He pressed his boot against her cheekbone and waited for her to talk but she kept silent.

'Do you know the force of what you are dealing with? Do you know how small you are, *zama lur*, underneath me?'

She could not open her mouth to speak. Samarra twitched, indicating that she wanted to talk, that she had something to say. He removed his boot from her face, but her hair, fanned out on the floor, pulled at her scalp as his feet readjusted themselves. Samarra licked the inside of her cheek. She tasted the dirt of the floor.

'I know who you are.'

Her voice was quieter than she imagined, as if she still had the rag over her mouth suffocating her.

The man smiled. He played with a wedding ring on his left hand. She saw it for the first time as he twirled it once and then counter-clockwise twice, as though he was opening the combination to a safety deposit box. She waited for him to twist it a third time.

'I know that you are the ones who have sold everything in this country you defend so urgently. You sold its gold, its oil, its coal, its harbours. I know you are the first in these sixty-six years of your great country's history to have sold its skies. What have you left untouched?'

Samarra's voice rose. She felt her strength return, she even thought she could hear the blood rushing against her right ear.

'Who are you to sell the sky?'

His face contorted. His wedding ring stopped its twirl. His hands fell to his sides. With her one eye that was not closed against the dark crevice between her face and the floor, she saw him lunge towards her. His hands closed upon her face and he pulled her off the ground, her neck straining, her body falling loose so that the pain of what came next would be lessened by her weaker resistance. Having lifted Samarra, the army man held her against the wall, his palms against her forehead, her neck. She promised herself that she would not cry; she promised herself, as she began to feel her eyes burn, that she would not scream.

'Bring the boys in.'

He issued the command and released her. He didn't look at Samarra as he picked his pistol off the chair he had been sitting on and tucked it back into his holster, clicking the safety catch shut, before walking out of the room.

After she had been let go, she tried to clean herself up in the home of a friend so that her mother would not see what they had done to her. After Samarra realized that what they had done could not be cleaned up, not erased or lightened with soap and make-up, she called her mother and told her that she was spending the night at her friend's home. The room was dark except for the halo of light coming from the TV, switched on to one of the many talk shows aired at night. The volume was low and Samarra couldn't hear the presenter. Malalai could barely hear her daughter on the line.

Samarra touched her cheek. His ox-blood boots had left an impression on her face. Torn skin, purple bruises, a constellation of tiny broken capillaries. Samarra held the phone away from her ear. The sound of her mother's voice hurt. She could feel the blood rushing against her temples.

It was only this time, she promised her mother; it was late and she did not want to travel alone at night – you never knew how safe you were in Mir Ali, Samarra reminded her. And Malalai, fearfully aware, agreed and relented.

Her second call had been to Aman Erum. Samarra dialled his number and, in the clearest English she could muster, she asked the American boy who picked up the phone if she could speak to Aman Erum. It took Aman Erum four minutes to come on the line – no one called him at his hostel, he used the phone at his discretion. And though he had given people in Mir Ali the number in case of emergencies, this was the first call he had received from home.

When Samarra heard his voice she began to cry. She had forbidden herself any tears until then. But with Aman Erum, Samarra let go. She sobbed, he thought he heard her howl. Ghazan, Ghazan Afridi. He thought he heard her say her father's name. And me. And now me. But her cries tore through the line. It took Aman Erum some time to understand what Samarra was trying to say to him. At first he couldn't make out the words; they were strangled in her throat and he couldn't understand what she was saying except for *zalim*. Between her growling cries she repeated the word over and over. The unjust. The injustice. When he understood, when Aman Erum finally understood what Samarra had been saying, he dropped the phone.

Aman Erum stands on the pavement quietly, thinking about what he is about to do. He looks behind once more to make sure he hasn't been followed. Though half of him hopes that Colonel Tarik has been trailing him all this time. Aman Erum

168

half hopes that the Colonel will catch him and stop him. He looks at his watch. There isn't much time left. He has to reach the agreed-upon spot and make the call. Prayers are at noon. He has less than an hour left.

17

Sikandar keeps his eyes on the Talib speaking to each other. He can see them arguing. When they catch his eye, he lowers his gaze. Mina is deathly still. She has not moved since the man with the light-blue turban backed away from her window. Mina places her hands on her lap and talks to her husband under her breath. Unlike him, she does not lower her eyes. She does not bow her head. She keeps her head upright and looks straight ahead at the unrecognizable wilderness of the forest around them.

'What are you doing?'

Sikandar can't answer. He shakes his head slightly, too slightly. Mina doesn't see the movement. She hasn't turned to look at him.

'What are you doing to get us out of this?'

As her voice quickens, her teeth bite against each other.

Sikandar tries to answer. He wants to tell her everything is going to be all right, to look at this as a checkpoint – they have been through hundreds, thousands, of them before – this is no different, only the toll is unusual. But nothing comes out. He shakes his head again. It seems to move on its own, like the nervous tremble of a hummingbird. His neck tightens.

'Mina –'

She turns towards him, breaking her posture.

'*Kha*, say something.'

'I'm sorry . . .'

He sees her shoulders slump forward before she straightens herself upright in defiance of the betrayal her body feels. He hears her inhale angrily, quickly. Sikandar watches Mina's body stiffen again. She turns her torso away from him and towards the dashboard.

'I'm sorry.'

She closes her ears to him. She moves her handbag off her lap, putting it first between her thighs and the door, crowding her seat, then reconsiders. What if the Talib suspect she's getting too comfortable? Mina folds the bag so it takes up less space, and just then Sikandar hears the sound again. Beads rolling against each other. He's almost certain it's beads.

He listens, not lifting his eyes, for the tapping sound the invisible objects make as they clink against each other in Mina's moving bag. For the first time that day, he hears the noise clearly. What does she have hidden in there? Sikandar counts the rings on Mina's fingers: all there. He checks the buttons on her cardigan absent-mindedly. He allows his eyes to graze along his wife's body before he closes them.

Tamarind seeds.

Counted at funerals. The words of prayers said over them before they're offered as petitions to God on the behalf of the deceased. She carries them with her.

Sikandar turns his face slightly to look at Mina. Their son had looked like his mother in profile. Small nose, high bones that were almost Mongoloid, silken hair. Hers is now brittle and growing white from neglect. Zalan had looked very little like him. He had not grown old enough to develop the heavier features of his father. But he had been frightened like him. They had their fear in common. Sikandar's heart sinks with the memory of his son's inheritance.

For a brief time, when the nights were longer, Zalan was all Sikandar's. He sat in his father's silhouette and did not leave him until he closed his eyes for sleep. It was Sikandar who put Zalan to bed with a short story and three kisses, one extra for good luck.

Sikandar has not thought of those nights for some time. He

has stopped his mind from wandering to his son. Sitting with Mina in the van, Sikandar prays for nothing more than quiet so that he can revisit those long-ago evenings.

To him, Zalan always remained that sleepy, frightened but proud boy. He pictures his son, no matter how old, as that unsure little boy.

'I'm too afraid to close my eyes, Baba,' Zalan would say, the furry blanket pulled up to his chin, its stray hairs getting caught in his mouth and eyelashes. Zalan would have to free his hands to clear them off.

'Why?' his father would ask gently.

'When I close my eyes at night,' Zalan would reply, 'I have bad dreams.'

'Close your eyes and summon two lions,' Sikandar would say, his voice so clear with authority that his son sat up to listen. 'Think of them as statues, as gatekeepers. They will guard the ministries and buildings of your dreams.'

That was all Zalan needed. Comforted by the lions, his own invented guardians, Zalan would drift to sleep in the crook of his father's shoulder.

Sikandar's eyes sting with tears.

The men break apart and return to their positions surrounding the van, Kalashnikovs cushioned in their arms and pointed at the driver's seat. The gaunt commander speaks with a new tremor in his voice.

'Are you a Muslim?'

Sikandar bows his head as he turns towards his window. 'Yes, yes,' he says, and nods in confirmation. 'Yes, of course, I am a Muslim.'

The Talib wraps his shawl round his neck, freeing his arms which had struggled against the fabric as he rammed the gun into Sikandar's face earlier.

'You are a man of the faith?'

Sikandar feels foolish now. He has worried over nothing, over an imagined fear these young boys can't inspire, not even with assault rifles draped over their shoulders.

The rain, which had let up briefly for the last half an hour, returns. Water falls on the gaunt Talib's threadbare *kameez*. The wet tunic clings to his skin. It is transparent. Mina thinks she can see the outline of a T-shirt underneath. She sees light colours, faded from wear, shades of yellow and green. She thinks she can see a silhouette of the man on the shirt: Bob Marley. Mina looks at her feet.

'Yes, yes, of course. I am driving the doctor to the village where she is needed and then I will be returning for my prayers.'

Sikandar smiles at the gaunt Talib, encouraging solidarity. He smiles cautiously, in anticipation of the positive response his prayers will elicit. The Talib does not return the gesture.

Mina breathes quietly in her seat. She shuts her eyes for the first time and focuses on the men's voices. Sikandar looks at her for approval, for her to issue an apology to him now. She was wrong to doubt him. But he sees that her forehead is still tight, her skin pinched into deep lines. He can hear her teeth grind against each other.

'You fold your arms when you pray, *drever –*'

Sikandar doesn't let him finish his sentence uninterrupted. This is a misunderstanding. He hurriedly assures the Talib of his right intentions and his journey on the right path.

'Brother, *ror*, I am a Muslim. I pray each week. I was first taken for *munz* by my father as a young boy. I learned how to speak to God before I could write. I taught my own son, my own boy, how to give thanks. I pray today for the blessing of Eid.'

The gaunt Talib pushes his gun into the car, stabbing Sikandar's shoulder.

'I asked you a question. Answer it.'

Sikandar's wan smile is cast off by the burn of the Kalashnikov's muzzle against his *kameez*. It's hot; it has only just been fired.

'I'm sorry, I'm sorry, *ror*. I misunderstood.'

'I asked you if you were a Muslim.'

Sikandar answers carefully, 'I am. I was five years old when I first said the *kalma*.'

'You don't hear me, *drever*. How many times do you pray?'

Sikandar doesn't want to reveal himself as a once a week, once a month – truthfully, once or twice every year – supplicant but if he lies and says he prays daily they might know. They have men everywhere these days, especially in the mosques, who might out him as a sinner, as a liar. Sikandar weighs the two against each other. There is redemption afforded to lax believers. There is none for liars.

'I am . . .'

Sikandar starts, but he can't say the words with Mina looking at him. He feels her glare upon him. She knows he is a coward.

'I am only a driver . . . I do not have the time to live as a good Muslim must . . . I pray on Fridays whenever I am able to leave work for a few moments . . .'

The Talib turns the gun with one swift revolution and rams the butt of the rusted Kalashnikov against Sikandar's temple.

'*Chap sha!* Shut up! You think this is a joke?'

Sikandar holds up his hands. There is blood on his white *kameez*. Droplets of rich red are falling onto his lap from somewhere, but he can't feel where the gun has cut him. His face, his head, his neck and shoulder all feel heavy and bruised. He licks his gums. There is no blood in his mouth. He inhales the rich scent of the air, sweetened by pine cones.

'Do you pray three times a day?'

Sikandar understands now, his meditation interrupted, that it is his eyebrow. The skin above his left brow has been ripped open. His eye stings and he blinks quickly to avoid the blood falling into his eye.

'Brother, I am sorry. I do not pray daily, but I will. I will.'

Sikandar promises blindly, eagerly. They can't beat him for that. The gaunt commander looks at the Talib back at his position guarding Mina's window. He nods at him and the Talib lifts his automatic weapon to place it against Mina's head. The gaunt Talib leans his body against the van so that his torso is bent over into Sikandar's window.

'*Khar bachaya.*'

He whispers the curse at Sikandar.

'Are you Sunni or Shia?'

18

Samarra had gone to Hayat when Aman Erum stopped calling her. She could not understand, especially after what had happened, why he no longer called her in the mornings and woke her up with the shrill ring of the phone. Samarra did not understand what had happened to the boy who used to wait for her by the screen door, hobbling over to her, dragging the dead leg that had fallen asleep under his books as he counted the minutes till her footsteps sounded on the pebbles outside his house.

Aman Erum never answered when she called his hostel any more. In the beginning, whoever answered the phone would return after a couple of minutes and tell her in a distracted voice that Aman Erum wasn't around. But later on, as her calls grew more frequent and more needy, no one even bothered to come back to the phone; they just left her dangling, like the receiver, without answer.

Samarra waited for a letter, a postcard, an envelope containing a museum ticket, a cinema stub. But Aman Erum wouldn't send a word. Samarra walked past his house in the evenings, hiding her face in the twilight, and looked into the driveway, searching for a sign that something else was wrong. She could not bring herself to talk to his family. Not like this, not with the welt of a smart ox-blood army boot still on her face. But night after night, Samarra saw no extra lights, no bodies moving about hurriedly, nothing.

To her mother, Samarra feigned an accident. It had been so long since she drove a motorbike, she said. Malalai, unable to hear any reference to Ghazan Afridi without tears, asked no more. But everyone else stared. They looked at her with worry and with fright. As if they knew.

Samarra sat in the Shah Sawar net café with her hair pulled across her face, and searched the world for news of New Jersey. But nothing. She remembered Aman Erum telling her of the café and of its underground curiosities. The men – there were only men at Shah Sawar, at the stations next to hers – moved their monitors. Some stood up and asked the proprietor for another place. Others just stared at the lone woman sitting at a computer with her hair falling over her eyes. She made them uncomfortable. She wasn't supposed to be there. But Samarra didn't care. She stared at her computer screen. Nothing. Samarra found no news of Aman Erum.

Samarra finally walked down the driveway and knocked on the screen door of the house on Sher Hakimullah road. She spoke to his mother, but Zainab was too kind to tell the girl that Aman Erum still called home, more often now, to speak to his brothers about his studies and to hear the local news of the town.

'I don't understand what I have done,' Samarra said as she sat at the kitchen table across from the old lady. She kept her eyes on the plastic tablecloth as she spoke.

Samarra was unused to Zainab. It was Inayat she knew from her summer holidays with Ghazan Afridi, but he was on bed rest now. She could not disturb him.

'Did uncle say anything?' she asked hopefully. Zainab shook her head no. 'When Aman Erum left, when he was preparing to leave, he told me he was going for us.' Samarra was embarrassed by the declaration. She remembered the walk down the deserted alleyways behind the mosque that night. She could smell the laundry drip-drying above their heads. 'Has he . . .' Samarra didn't know what to ask Zainab. She tried to hide behind her hands, which she raised to cover her mouth as she spoke. 'Has he changed his plans?'

Hayat stood in the corridor outside the kitchen. He had overheard Samarra's voice and had come to sneak a glance, but Samarra didn't resemble the woman he remembered as a boy. He remembered watching her from a window by the staircase. Hayat had watched as Samarra sat with Aman Erum outside the house, laughing and pulling his cheek in her thumb and forefinger, teasing him as she towered over him as a gangly teenaged girl. She had always been beautiful. She was something else now – she seemed anxious, afraid. But Hayat could see that Samarra was working hard to hide her anger. He watched her as she picked at the dry skin on her lips and spoke to Zainab.

Zainab ignored the worry in Samarra's voice and poured the tea, waving away her concerns. You know how the young are, you know how busy, how far away, how difficult, how many responsibilities. But Samarra was not swayed. Hayat could see it from the corridor.

'I cannot be left again –' Samarra started then stopped. Zainab waited for Samarra to finish; she could not guess what lay at the end of the sentence as she got up to rummage for some honey to pour into the tea. 'I cannot be left again without –'

'Without what, *bachaya*?'

'I cannot . . .' Samarra's back swelled with every breath she took.

Hayat could not bear to hear her say it. Zainab returned with the honey and comforted Samarra by lying, patting her hands – scratched by the open wire of her silver thread – and saying that Aman Erum must have been very busy and not to worry. But when Samarra left the house that day, begging leave from Zainab and bolting out through the front door, Hayat followed her. She had lost weight. Her long hair looked heavy framing her drawn face. Her nails were peeled down to their half-moons. Her lips were bitten and spotted with dry skin and blood. Hayat offered to drive her home on his motorbike.

Samarra felt strange, sitting behind Aman Erum's younger brother. He was younger, but even as a child he had been taller than his brother. She had played cricket with him when he was small. She didn't want him to see her like this, confused, bedraggled. She had never been this person, not even when she was seventeen.

She shook her head now so that her long hair moved across her back – she refused to wear a helmet although Hayat had one that he never wore, storing it under the seat, and which he'd offered her out of politeness.

Hayat didn't say anything till they were driving.

'He calls, you know.'

Samarra straightened her posture from a side-saddle slump and waited for him to continue. Hayat had almost hoped his words would get lost amongst the sounds of traffic that afternoon. But still he said them. For a brief second Samarra held Hayat's waist tightly.

'What does he say?'

'What he always does: very little. We do the talking mostly. But he still calls.'

Samarra did not cry, she never cries. She simply nodded and rested her face against Hayat's back.

From then on they started talking. Hayat would drive Samarra home from university, to friends' houses, to pick up fruit from the market. He never left her alone. At first, Samarra didn't tell him what had happened to her. She would not place those seven hours of her life. She wished to leave them behind, to re-time her days so that those hours fell off the clock. But he understood. Hayat understood that the more she wanted to lose those hours, the more they followed her.

Aman Erum misunderstood how entrenched Samarra had been. He had thought her to be a pivotal character of some sort, but she wasn't. She had been a shadow courier – telling this person to leave that safe house, visiting a commander's mother to bring her food and money while her son or husband was in hiding, taking notes on timings to be coded and then decoded. Errands. Samarra had run intelligence errands. She had not been central. She was inconsequential. But Aman Erum drove her deeper into the movement; it was where she sought her protection after those vanished seven hours.

His brother, Hayat, had been central. Hayat hadn't spoken a word, hadn't said anything tantalizing to Aman Erum on the phone – that should have been the tip-off. Aman Erum should have pressed him, but he didn't. He knew Hayat was popular at university, that he quietly attended protests and demonstrations as if he were merely an observer, rather than a participant. He knew where Hayat had learned his loyalties. He forgave no one their trespasses upon Mir Ali.

Hayat stepped in and took care of Samarra. He comforted her over his brother's cruel absence and saw how deeply she had absorbed her father's fury. As they grew closer, Hayat encouraged her to go back to the work she had been doing, back to the men she had couriered for. He spoke to them on her behalf. Samarra could not be doubted. She reported right back to duty and wasted no time in exacting her revenge.

'Ghazan Afridi is never coming back,' she said to Hayat as she sat behind him on the motorbike one night. 'They have had him for over seventy thousand unaccounted hours.' Hayat listened, hoping she had not really counted. 'Seventy thousand and eighty hours,' Samarra said, her voice steady. After years of enduring other people's empty hope – he will return eventually. Won't he? He must – she finally had her answer confirmed.

Samarra replaced the men as they fell. She replaced them even when they did not fall. She had become, in the short time that such revolutionary movements allow, being short on time themselves, a leading figure in the battle of Mir Ali.

Hayat had watched her grow, watched her fear slip away into other rooms. He could not have been more encouraging of her. Eventually, even he took his orders from her. He never struggled against her, never questioned her expanding powers. When she moved their meetings away from the open university grounds, where they had assumed the pose of students picnicking innocently under the shaded sun, to the dark tower of the history department Hayat did not ask why she had brought them to their place.

He had first held her there, closing her in his arms as she spoke about that seven-hour day. Samarra stood with her back against the door and told Hayat about the man with the ox-blood boots. Without raising her voice an octave, she told him about the hours that passed before the men let themselves out of the room. She spoke in short sentences. She did not cry. But she did not move her back from the door either. She didn't leave herself unguarded. Hayat gave Samarra her space. Strands of her hair clung to the door with static as she delivered her précis. Hayat listened quietly, but he knew she was holding back. He could feel her retreat, saw her shiver as she mouthed certain words. Hayat was almost certain he saw her shiver. Ox-blood boots. Hayat moved closer to Samarra in the empty classroom in the dark tower.

It had been their place.

Their dark tower.

Hayat had first kissed her in that very building.

There was no language for it. Hayat had stood before Samarra in the shadows of the dark tower, nervous. There were eyes everywhere in Mir Ali; people watched you even as you slept, as you dreamed. No conversation was safe from listeners who intruded upon every fleeting thought. Hayat could not say what he felt. He only wanted to be near Samarra, to protect her, to smell the jasmines that had once left their perfume lingering on her wrists.

He said her name, softly. She raised her face to look at him. Samarra tried not to blink. She did not want to stop him, but she was scared. She closed her eyes. Hayat moved closer to her. He couldn't think clearly. He could only see this stolen moment, robbed from Mir Ali where there was no space for secrets such as these, and Samarra. Samarra with the beauty mark in her eye. He said her name over and over to himself, quietly, until he built the courage to lift her chin to meet his lips.

Hayat had been so anxious, he had paused three seconds too long, the length of two Samarras, silently repeated. In the delay, Samarra opened her eyes. Hayat bent his head and kissed Samarra's forehead, then her eyes, both left and right, and when she did not flinch Hayat finally kissed her lips.

She brought the meetings here eleven months later. To this very room. She had packed the floor with hunchbacks and positioned herself away from the door.

Hayat deferred to Samarra's cool judgement more often than he imposed his own. But she had changed in other ways as well. She had hardened. It had happened much too quickly. She became too ambitious. She was no longer, not in any seriously debilitating way, afraid of what might happen to her.

At times she told herself that her imaginings of what more they were capable of doing to her were far worse than what had actually happened. She had endured only seven hours of them, of their power over her. What was that to a lifetime of fear? If they caught her now, what was the worst they could do? Fourteen hours? Twenty-one?

(Seventy thousand and eighty hours. She was no longer afraid of her calculations.)

She bargained with numbers she had no control over. Samarra hid from her memories by driving herself deeper into what they had punished her for. She would never be afraid of them, of the man with the wedding ring, again. Samarra had taken precautions this time. There was no one Samarra loved enough to protect from the consequences of her actions. She had cut those ties and loosened those attachments.

This made her dangerous.

Samarra never suspected this was a battle she could not win. It made her reckless.

'Samarra,' Hayat says gently, 'this will change everything. You know that. You can stop it – you can still change the plan.' Hayat runs his hands through his hair, holding the soaked Chitrali pakol in his fist.

She smiles. She's not listening to him. He lowers his hands. He doesn't know how to reach her any more.

'You know you will never be able to go home again – are you prepared for that? You're ready for your life to be taken with the Chief Minister's?'

Samarra smiles again. She hasn't taken her eyes off him.

'What life, Hayat *jan*?'

11:06

19

He can't answer. If he tells them, they will execute him.

People coming from Peshawar spoke of drive-by shootings, of men in parrot-green turbans who rode pillion on motor-bikes and sidled up next to the cars of well-known Shia businessmen at red traffic lights and opened fire. They gunned down unknown businessmen too – the shopkeepers, the small-time spice traders and glass merchants – in the smoggy city's bazaars.

It had already spread far and wide, this green-turbaned movement, before the Talib gave them international recognition. In the years before the Talib assumed the mountainside the attacks had not been confined to Peshawar. In Karachi there had been the dark years of targeted assassination campaigns against Shia doctors. By the end of a decade, they had murdered almost two hundred of them. Doctors emigrated in large numbers to Canada and Europe from the country's other urban capitals, unable to practise their professions or their faiths in safety.

In Quetta they attacked religious processions, killing the faithful in their mosques on their most holy and sorrowful of days. In Multan they planted bombs in the parks and alleyways near people's homes. They pulled children out of school buses and slit their throats on the roadsides. They murdered men ostensibly to level a millennium-old quarrel over succession, over dynastic rights, armed only with the defensive guilt of those who had usurped a power that was not theirs to take.

Sikandar is not a religious man. He does not have the mark

of prostration on his forehead like many Shias do, marks of devotion from the carved tablets they place on their prayer mats so that their faces are imprinted by the continual soar and surge of their daily orisons. He doesn't carry too obvious a name, nothing that could betray his family's following of that correct line of succession. He doesn't believe in second comings and long-awaited prophets; at the very least he does not think too much about it.

But he is a Shia. In name and in birth. That is enough.

Sikandar raises his palms together and bows his head to the gaunt commander.

'Brother, I am just a Muslim. Please let me go.'

'We do not consider infidels members of the tribe.'

The gaunt Talib grows heartier, less anaemic-looking, as he breathes in the exclusive power of his faith. He grips his gun like a sabre, threatening to bring it down over Sikandar, before barking: 'If you are not a Shia declare it! Who are you hiding your pride from?'

Sikandar bows his head deeper. It is heavy with sweat and blood. Mina begins to mumble under her breath. He lets the blood rush to his ears so her mumblings are drowned out. She rocks back and forth gently in her seat. Sikandar hopes she isn't praying. He hopes there is nothing that can identify them as separate.

'I am not, brother. Please. I am not. I am a Muslim.'

In the silence, while his false confession is being considered, while the Talib exchange aggravated glances with one another, Sikandar offers a silent prayer.

He begs for release. He begs, as the thrum emanating from Mina grows louder, as he feels her body toughen with each oscillation of her shoulders, for her to remain calm. She is shaking now. She jerks her back off the seat and moans a low, guttural sound. They cannot survive an outburst right now. But it's God's timing, isn't it, for Mina's shallow calm to leave her just when it is most required. Mina beats her chest, her heart, with her open palm. He knows this moment. Sikandar knows that Mina will begin to speak. *Ya Ali, ya Ali*, she will mutter, saying the words to remember that she does not suffer alone. She will say them for strength, for solace. Don't say it, Mina. He squeezes his eyes tight. Please don't say it.

The thumping of her hand against her heart is enough. The Talibs can identify heresy through a palm. She groans the words. Sikandar hopes no one can understand them but him. She will get them killed. Mina has never hidden her faith, never lied for protection or for the comforts of assimilation.

The gaunt Talib steps to the front of the van to speak to one of his subordinates. Sikandar doesn't see him move; with his head hung low he barely registers any movement. The Talib returns now, backtracking three steps. He waves his gun at Sikandar.

'Take off your *kameez*,' he orders.

Sikandar can't process any of the Talib's thoughts. He doesn't understand his secret language of us versus us, of what makes you part of them and what makes you their enemy.

'Brother, I don't . . .'

'Don't call me brother!' the gaunt Talib shouts. He doesn't move his hand off the Kalashnikov, not even to wipe the falling drizzle from his sunburned cheekbones. The rain hangs off him like glycerine.

Sikandar gestures to Mina.

'I can't. Please.'

The Talib wants to see his back, wants to check if he has the marks of Ashura on his flesh. They want to see if he whipped a sword across his shoulder blades to commiserate with the pain the Holy Prophet's family felt as they were massacred at Karbala.

They want to know if he is one of the men who beat their palms across their chests, like Mina, until their skin is raw. If he is one of those who walk barefoot in processions across unswept streets, pricking their soles with shards of glass and thorns and still-lit cigarette butts.

Sikandar flinches in anticipation of another blow and he begins, in his nervous desperation, to sob. He has no consideration for the mother whose infant is being strangled by its umbilical cord, whose life he has come to this savage wilderness to save, and at that moment, for that cluster of seconds, he can spare no thought for his wife, who will never be able to look at her husband again. Sikandar sobs only for himself, for what he fears is about to happen in the coming minutes when his faith is confirmed and then condemned.

In one hour he has shamed himself more than months of Mina's hysteria have done. More than his body has ever allowed him to express in grief or in sadness it has let out in fear. He can't hold back. Sikandar's tears only anger the commander.

With the hand that doesn't have its index finger poised on the Kalashnikov's trigger, the Talib grabs Sikandar's hair and pulls his head back, holding him against the driver's seat. The gaunt Talib brings his face to within a centimetre of Sikandar's. Sikandar can smell him; he can smell the earth and the rain on the Talib's parched skin.

'*Kafir.*'

The Talib spits at him.

Sikandar can't breathe. He chokes on his tears.

The Talib tightens his hand on Sikandar's head. He straightens himself and chambers a round in the Kalashnikov. '*Kafir*,' he sneers once more. He is lifting the weapon to Sikandar's heart when he is interrupted by a scream.

It pierces through the light rain, through the tense breath that Sikandar allows his body to release, through the unshakeable anger of the Talib.

The gaunt commander's face contracts with the scream. Startled, he lets go of Sikandar, whose hair falls out of his clenched fist, and looks at his comrades.

Mina has got out of the van. She opened her door and pushed the Talib with the wispy beard and light-blue turban, who was stationed next to her window. She pushed him hard, touching him against all convention, placing her hands flat on his body and straining her arms to push him as forcefully as her strength would allow. Mina knocked him to the ground and out of her way. The Talib could not defend himself; he could not steady himself by grabbing hold of her wrists, so he fell. She barrelled her way past the man, the teenage boy, guarding the van's engine as if it too were an animate being, aiming his gun at the hood so he could shoot if the driver revved the van against his permission.

Mina screamed at him when he tried to stop her, and it was this scream that the commander heard.

'*Zalim!*' she screams, standing under the rain. Unjust! Mina screams till her voice is hoarse.

He moves. There is no greater slur Mina could have levelled. These men are students of justice. They can be accused of being violent, of being rash, of anything but injustice. They have built their war around the battle of the just against the unjust. People misunderstand them; they assume it's a war against unbelievers, against disbelief. That has nothing to do with it. Their war was always about justice. They bear its mantle and they drape themselves in its banner.

Mina strides towards the gaunt commander, holding her handbag in her hands. As she reaches him she drops it to the ground as if she only just remembered it, too late to leave it in the car. She self-consciously pulls on her *dupatta* and, confirming it remains round her neck, Mina shouts. She heaves air up from her lungs and screams.

20

Hayat kicks the earth with his foot. He doesn't want it to come to this. The soil he disturbs is tired. Fractured clumps of dirt unable to hold together.

He remembers a time, long ago, when he and his brothers were children. When one insurgency believed their harvest was ready to be reaped, when they felt that the moment was upon them, the feeling infected the town.

People prepared for change, for a reversal of forces and fortune, only to be beaten back harder, more viciously, as punishment for their daring. People laid low, but they did not feel that the harvest had been destroyed. It had simply not been ready. The moon was anxious, the orbit of the constellations falling into place required more time. So they waited.

They waited for one insurgency to pass and for another to take its place. With each battle for Mir Ali they held hope aloft and waited for the moment they would be free.

It never came. It never promised to come.

Hope stemmed purely from the belief that it ought to, that one day it just might.

For Inayat and his fellow men in arms the road to freedom was perilously long but they journeyed upon it confidently. Their losses in the face of superior military might, enhanced state powers and abuses, and national ignorance of their plight, fell off their shoulders. They lived and dreamed and died for the pursuit of that promise. That hope had been enough for them.

But not for Hayat. Not for the generation that came after

and saw their parents' dreams diminished, methodically squashed by the creation of larger and larger military cantonments where the army could teach schoolchildren how to sing the national anthem and where a larger perimeter of land flew the jungle-green and white flag of Pakistan atop their roofs and gates. The army beat this generation down by being bigger and stronger and faster. They beat them down by being exactly what this generation aspired to.

They wanted phones, computers, access to the world. The military had all those things waiting. Eventually the battle, as they had known, would come down to this: those who wanted to be a part of a global system would not be kept outside it on account of nationalistic beliefs and codes of honour set by their parents. Struggle would be redefined; it would come to mean the length of time you waited for fibre optic cables to be buried in the ground so that dial-up Internet could be replaced by something much, much smoother. This generation wanted scholarships, they wanted to travel for business degrees and seminars, to work at petrol pumps wearing bright orange jumpsuits in Eurozone countries if it meant the chance of a different life, one not ruled by checkpoints and national identity cards and suspicion. They wanted the freedom to travel to Mecca, business class.

It had only been a matter of time for the army. They had known that one day it would come to this. This was a lazy generation. The army had been counting on them. This generation, all spark and sound effects, quickly proved to be much easier than the army had imagined. Barring few exceptions, they didn't want to fight. They wanted too many things that only the state could give them. Their memories would still be infiltrated by the past, by their ancestors' grievances and sufferings, but they would recall these comfortably at dining tables and dinner parties as they wore the latest smartphones on their belts and compared their children's private school tuition fees.

They sacrificed nothing of their own; the dreams had been their fathers'.

Freedom meant nothing to this generation. It was easily bartered for convenience.

Hayat holds Samarra's dry hand in his. Little patches of cold and lack of care have whitened the skin around her knuckles and joints. He rubs her hand quickly with his own.

'With every escalation they hit us back harder.'

'We have always been hit,' she reminds Hayat, removing her hand from his.

'They will kill Nasir's family. If you give him the go-ahead, Samarra, they will trace him – whether he lives or dies – and they will torture his family for months before they make an example out of them.'

She is silent.

'They will leave no one. They won't spare his siblings, his nieces – his sister's two children. You know that. They will humiliate his father before they execute him here – on these very grounds. You know what they will do to his mother, Samarra, you above all people should know . . .'

Samarra stands up and walks away from Hayat. The cold makes her voice sound tremulous when it is not. Although her voice is clear and decisive, the sharp whistle of the rain makes her sound unsure.

'Stop it.'

Hayat lowers his head. He remembers his conversation with his mother in the kitchen this morning. His heart, he can feel his heart sinking.

'What's happened to you? What are you so afraid of?'

Hayat kicks the earth again and again with his foot.

'You don't see it, Samarra – you don't see it any more, do you?'

He burrows and digs his foot into the muddy soil. He can't stop her. She is so far gone she can't see anything beyond the white rage she has adjusted all her weight to carry, a rage that has grown to become a part of her. It is built into her like it was built into Ghazan Afridi, into Inayat, transforming itself virally, until Samarra has no immunity left to her anger.

She stares at Hayat, searching his face, waiting for it to break out into something familiar. She doesn't recognize him either. He's always been cautious on the eve of operations, treading lightly in the days and weeks beforehand, but there had been anticipation too. Eager anticipation.

'They've destroyed us.'

Samarra scoffs. She makes no effort to hide her reaction. Her voice sounds rough; there is a harshness to it. He can hear it, even in her sneers. Hayat ignores it. He ignores the way she tilts her head and looks up at him, as if she has not considered him before.

'We're no better than they are.'

But she won't let him finish the thought. Samarra shakes her hands at Hayat, waving him down, trying to stop him from starting down this path.

'Samarra,' he says.

This is not a meeting she can command.

'Samarra, listen to me. They killed our heroes, so we stopped making them.' His voice breaks. She can no longer see him; he knows she has already begun to drown him out. So he shouts. He shouts above the already too-loud decibel he speaks to her in. 'We stopped living. We stopped our lives to take theirs.'

Hayat looks at Samarra.

'We became them.'

Samarra sits back down again on the bare, wet earth, agitated.

'Hayat, that was before. This will change everything.'

Now she takes his hands, his also-cold hands in hers, and squeezes. Hayat looks at her hands. She must have rubbed them against her sweater, against the man's shawl thrown casually round her shoulders. He can't see the dry white patches any more. He looks up at her eyes, at the cold beauty mark encased in her iris, and wonders how she warmed her hands.

'This is what they couldn't do. They made our fathers old. They robbed our fathers of their youth, of their strength. They had no freedom to make their own rules. We are something stronger, Hayat. We are something that can't be broken.'

He shakes his head at her.

'Samarra, we already are.'

Samarra stands up and checks her phone, a black-plastic Nokia with a backlit screen whose light never fully turns off. She doesn't acknowledge Hayat's words. In their place, she carries on a conversation they never started.

'Let's go.'

Samarra presses two keys to unlock the phone and looks at the time. Nasir will be moving now. He will be preparing his position before the Chief Minister's motorcade blocks all the routes; he will be making his way to the venue as part of the late morning traffic, ahead of it becoming a high-security zone.

Hayat scrapes the dirt off his shoes. He can't stop her. He wonders if he tried hard enough. There's nothing left to do but to go ahead with the plan.

'We have things to prepare. Nasir will be waiting for my call on the other side.' Samarra moves her head as she speaks, reassuring herself as though ticking marks off a list. She checks her phone one more time. Hayat takes the keys out of his pocket.

'Enough battery?'

He knows Nasir won't move before Samarra's all-clear. She's

anxious now, worried her phone will fail her, concerned that all the elements will conspire against her. But she has three bars left on the mobile. Enough to make the call in an hour's time.

Samarra nods.

Hayat walks towards the motorbike.

'Let's go, then. We have things to prepare.'

She notices that he speaks to her over his shoulder. He doesn't even look at her.

21

Aman Erum makes his way on foot through the thinning traffic. He sidesteps boys on bicycles and harried husbands scurrying towards the stores to pick up last-minute packages of rice and sweetmeats before businesses shut for prayers and the Eid weekend ahead.

In Mir Ali's narrow bazaar, there are several butchers. Four or five at least that sit cross-legged on wooden slabs and tables sharpening their knives (which are not very sharp at all), while they snap orders to their child assistants: cut down two kilos of mutton; wrap up some fat; prepare the lamb hooves and bones for *paiya* – cooked slowly for hours and hours in a gelatinous sauce until you can nibble off just the right amount of cartilage and chew comfortably on what was once an animal's kneecap or knuckle.

Lamb skulls, deep pink and covered in flies, rest on the butchers' tables. They price the skulls for the jelly-like eyes, for the gristle of the cheek, for the marrow in the nose. Their clients don't mind the swarm of insects that crowd round the skulls or the flies that lay their eggs in the warm crevices of the lamb's face. The meat is easily cleaned out with warm water and lemon, a natural disinfectant.

Two of the butchers keep battery chickens nine to a cage, stacked high on top of each other, opening the rusted cages only to grab a hairless, featherless bird by its neck and cleave it into eatable parts. As a result it isn't the open ribbed carcasses or the dark-brown blood that slides down the butchers' tables and onto the streets that draws attention to the meat section of the market on Eid morning, but the shrieks of the confined birds. Their skin is crusty and scabbed from repeated attempts at escaping their wiry enclosures. They squawk desperately, constantly moving in their cages and flapping their wings, as though it were possible for them to knock down the tower in which their cages are placed, and lift themselves off the ground and upwards into the cloudy sky.

Aman Erum walks amongst the morning's late risers, keeping track of the time. The drizzle continues. It has barely let up all morning. Now, just before noon, it is a light sprinkling of rainwater that falls timidly, sliding down the windscreens of passing cars and the arms of men wearing crisply starched *shalwar kameez*.

It's been a long time since Aman Erum was in Mir Ali on Eid. He missed the holiday when he was abroad studying. When he returned to be with Inayat as his father's lungs filled with fluid, Aman Erum was determined to be with his family for Eid. He wouldn't leave them for Eid again. At first he imagined he would come home for the holiday, returning to New Jersey as soon as his father's mourning period had ended, but his family needed him. They needed someone with a steady hand to guide them; it had been such a difficult year. Coming back from America with his overseas contacts and local connections, Aman Erum was a new man. He would return to America eventually, once he had built up certain supply chains he had been working on, but until then Mir Ali would be where he spent his late Eid nights, trawling the markets, and his Eid mornings, bowed down among the bodies of those who gave blessings for a new year.

Aman Erum passes the chicken coops and sees the almost hairless birds beating their wings against their wire cages. If everything goes well today, he will buy two of the fattest to take home.

He will ask his mother to cook them with butter and red chilli powder, the sweetest variety of which comes from Kashmir. When he was in New Jersey, Aman Erum went to Indian restaurants, to small canteens where taxi drivers and migrants huddled under dim lighting and listened to scratchy recordings of old film tunes, sung in the days of black and white Bollywood cinema, to eat the dish.

Aman Erum walks faster as he notices the time, quickening his step while making sure not to trip in the small puddles that have collected in the fissures and fractures of the city's unpaved streets. The rickshaw drivers honk their horns at him: would he like a ride? Aman Erum waves a hand in the air, no, and then places it over his heart in thanks. The morning's anxiety lifts off him. After all these years he sees an end in sight. He'll be free of this soon. There is no other way. It has come to this after much struggle. Aman Erum's heart hurts at the thought of what he must do, but there is simply no other way. Someone has to make the violence, the constant threat of it, stop. A steady hand is required. He has no other choice.

One of the rickshaws slows down and the driver stretches his thinly shirted body out of the vehicle.

'*Agha*, you are going far. Let me drive you.'

Aman Erum looks at the decal on the rickshaw's plastic roof: a map sawn and torn. *May God steal from you what you have taken from Him*. It's a line from a poem. Aman Erum hops into the back of the rickshaw, its rain-proofed seat covers ripped from wear.

'*Mehrabani*,' Aman Erum thanks the driver, his hand still resting over his heart.

They drive past the bazaar as the shop's shutters fall in unison. Aman Erum averts his eyes as they pass the Haji Abdullah Shirazi Khan slums, broken-down shacks leaning over one another, like ants crowding for space. He tries not to breathe in the fumes of the sputtering exhaust. He holds out a palm and measures the space between each raindrop. He thinks of Zalan and how the little boy used to cup his palms to catch the rain, squeezing his eyes shut as he tilted his head towards the sky. This morning will be over soon. It will all be over soon.

The rickshaw driver stops just outside the Hussain Kamal street mosque, its garden still free of the plastic *chappals* that will soon be scattered everywhere, haphazardly. It's early. The Friday congregation has not begun to arrive yet. There is time.

Aman Erum thanks the driver, who refuses his money once and then twice, and gets out of the rickshaw. He looks around him, there's little movement, almost no traffic. A roadblock is being set up nearby.

Aman Erum walks to a small *hotal*. Long, splintered wooden tables are spread out in the pattern of cafeteria seating and are lined with blue plastic chairs. A man stands on a raised platform, stirring a large saucepan of tea, throwing in sugar by the palmful. Further away, in front of a tandoor oven, a man in a blackened apron pulls out fluffy *rotay* with his uncovered hands, dropping the hot bread onto metal platters before his fingers burn.

Aman Erum sits down at one of the tables at the front, keeping his distance from the others who have gathered here to eat a late breakfast. Men huddle together dipping chunks of hot bread into their sweetened tea, swallowing their soggy meal before the mosques sing the call of the midday *azan*.

Looking across the street, turning his head both ways and seeing no one, Aman Erum orders a cup of tea. He drinks it slowly, blowing air over the milky skin on top. Light-brown film has already begun to cling to the sides of the chipped plastic mug. After scalding his tongue, he beckons the server boy over.

'*Sa taim dey?*'

The boy has the soft features of those who live in the border town. Hair lightened by sun and wind, and fine, breakable bones. He dries his hands on his stained *shalwar* and tilts his head towards the small colour TV hung under the ceiling's yellow tube lights, unlit this early in the day. 'It's after eleven,' the delicate server boy says, squinting to read the time.

Aman Erum looks past the boy. He hasn't arrived yet.

He takes out his mobile phone and places it on the table before him. With one eye on the road he punches in the numbers. All he has to do now is press the button.

11:39

22

The server boy with the fine bones and a small rash along his chin comes back over to Aman Erum's table with a wide plastic tray gingerly balanced on his bony hip. Aman Erum hasn't noticed the rash before; it's so light it might have been caused by heat from the tandoor fire. The server boy lifts a metallic plate laden with hot, buttered *rotay* off his tray, and places it before Aman Erum, bending at the knees to avoid putting the plate down too hard. He moves around Aman Erum's chair and lays down another plate: deep-fried liver cooked in its juices and garnished with thinly cut slices of soft tomato.

'The boss sent this over.'

The server boy turns his head towards the man underneath the fourteen-inch TV screen, thumbing through receipts written on scraps of paper stapled together.

'Said *agha* deserves a proper breakfast. You will starve on just a cup of tea.'

Aman Erum raises his hand in greeting and makes to stand up to thank the proprietor, who waves him back down, patting the air with his palms. He points to himself and then the table – he will come to him in five minutes' time. Aman Erum smiles and sits down again, checking the road once more as he does so.

He dips his bread into the watery juice the cubes of liver float in and places it in his mouth, sucking on it for a moment and savouring the taste before rolling the lump of bread over to his teeth. He barely ate this morning, and he hadn't realized how hungry he was till now. The stress of his ill-timed meeting with the Colonel drifts over him as the morning minutes tick closer to noon.

Aman Erum's hunger suddenly feels urgent and he wolfs down the soft, smoke-flavoured bites until he notices his hands are shaking. He slows down, putting his hands on the table as the server boy brings a cold metal tumbler of water. Aman Erum picks up the water and drinks greedily.

It has unfortunately come to this.

He tells himself there is no other way, no other way to be free of the Colonel, of his pain. It had been only his and then, without warning, it had infected his whole family. In his absence, the violence had grown. Upon his return, it had met him at home. Aman Erum is hungry and he is tired but he must be clear about his intentions. He looks at his hands. They rest on the table. He lifts his right hand; it is perfectly still.

Since he returned to Mir Ali, Aman Erum has done well for himself. Though he returned out of duty to his father and had planned to stay only the necessary amount of time, Aman Erum has benefited from his delayed return to America. He's made a name in his business – one that will come with financial advantages when he does go back to America. He has brought comfort to his family during their difficult hours, and he has returned to guide Hayat. But belonging, especially to such ravaged soil, involves much sacrifice.

Aman Erum imagines that his sacrifices would not have been demanded elsewhere. His limited exposure to the rest of the country has told him that the others live well enough. Mir Ali pays the price for the comfort of those strangers; Mir Ali and its men have paid for decades.

'*Agha!*' The *hotal* owner clasps his hands together. 'It is an honour to serve you here.'

Aman Erum wipes his hands free from the *rotay*'s yeast and shakes the proprietor's hand.

'What a place you have here, boss. I would have come much earlier but it has been very hectic at home.'

The man bobs his head sympathetically.

'Of course, of course. You are a pillar of our community. On top of the difficulties of your family's recent tragedies, you must be overburdened with work, *agha*. We are happy to see you and, please, let me know if ever there is anything I can do for you.'

He takes a pen out of his *kameez* breast pocket and writes down a number on one of the scraps of paper that no longer serve as receipts.

'I would be honoured to send something for your family on Eid. Please tell someone to call me tomorrow and I will have a parcel of our *kheer* ready to be picked up.'

Aman Erum thanks him and asks for his bill, which is immediately refused. 'Please, you are my guest,' he is told by the offended *hotal* owner. Aman Erum smiles, showing his teeth, and places his hand over his heart once more in sincere thanks.

He wipes his hands again on the slip of paper he has just been handed and sits back down to drink his tea, which has only just cooled. Aman Erum thinks of Eid, of the rest of the day and the deliverance it will bring. Looking across the road, Aman Erum sees him reach.

The enormous weight he has carried all morning bears down on his shoulders. Aman Erum's heart beats fast, so loudly that it drowns out the sounds of the *hotal*. He can no longer hear the slap of the dough on the counter, not the scrape of the *rotay* being pulled out of the tandoor, not the pouring of cups and cups of tea. Everything falls silent. It is time. He is here; they have arrived.

Aman Erum picks up his mobile phone and presses the green button.

23

The gaunt commander holds his weapon between him and Mina, desperate to keep a barrier between them, but she beats through it. Screaming, she pounds his chest, unconcerned by the Kalashnikov he wears as protection.

'*Zalim! Der zalim aye! Bey insaf!*'

She cries out all the names she knows to speak of what these men have done. She cries as she thrashes her fists across the Talib's sinewy chest.

'*Khaza –*' Woman. He tries to interrupt her, to remind her of her place and their space but nothing can reach Mina now. Her kohl eyeliner has all but vanished from the rims of her eyes as she cries through her words.

'It was you, it was your men, your men who took him from us. He hadn't done anything. He hadn't even begun to live. He wore his shoes till his toes pushed against them, growing too fast for him to notice. He had blisters on those toes. I saw them. I kissed them, touching each toe to my lips, when I went to identify him. Do you have any shame? Do you have any shame in the face of the mothers you have robbed of their boys?'

Not a noise passes between the Talib.

The one at the front of the van raises an eyebrow at the man Mina slammed herself against. His *shalwar* is covered in rainwater and mud. As he lifts himself off the ground, embarrassed, he hits his thighs, trying to clean himself, as though cleanliness will blot out the fall. But he can't see how dirty he is. He has mud round his ears. He slaps his thighs angrily, quickly, as he stands.

She is mad. They communicate this to each other with their eyes. The woman is crazy. Let her scream, we'll overpower her once she exhausts herself. The gaunt Talib takes a step back, away from Mina. She takes a step forward, unwilling to let him go.

When she slid out of the van, Sikandar hadn't even heard the click of the door handle. He had only heard the Talib's grunts as he grabbed Sikandar by the hair and held him against the driver's seat. In those seconds he had not heard Mina leave him, he had barely heard her scream, imagining that he had made the sound. When the commander let go of his head, releasing his grip on Sikandar as aggressively as he had first grabbed him, Sikandar slumped down in his seat and thanked God too quickly, too hopefully, thinking that he had been spared. When he turned to his wife's seat it was empty and, spinning back, he saw that there was no guard at his window. By the time he knew what was happening, by the time he understood that he had not been the screamer and that the noise had come from outside, Mina was in tears, shouting about their boy.

'Mina,' he whispers from his seat. 'Mina, what are you doing?'

She hears him. She turns angrily to Sikandar and glares at him. At that moment, Sikandar catches the eyes of the Talib. They understand. They look at her like she's infectious, like her delirium has been brought on by no fault of their own. From the way she responds to the feeble driver, the weary Talib know they have an unhinged woman on their hands. There is no use fighting her back; she is hysterical. The Talib wait patiently, standing perfectly still, while Mina rages, hitting and scratching the breast of the commander.

'He was there on a Saturday, visiting his father.'

Mina turns back to the window where Sikandar sits, throwing her arms in his direction. Freeing the Talib for a second, she turns and says those words at Sikandar as if they scorch her throat.

Sikandar feels his eyes well with tears.

'Mina,' he whispers again. 'Mina, don't tell them.'

'He had been going there since he was a child, going to the hospital to sit with the nurses who always gave him their time, taking him during their off-duty hours to buy ice cream. He had no school, he had no school that day, and so he went to see his father.'

Mina's voice cracks as her volume rises.

'You didn't care. You didn't care who was in there. You didn't even stop to think of the boys.'

The gaunt Talib has had enough. Now he holds his Kalashnikov between his two hands like a shield and pushes Mina with it.

'*Chap sha!*'

He raises his voice far above Mina's. She stumbles, one foot hitting the other with the force of the blow. Her sandal slips off her right heel.

'Shut your mouth. We are the protectors of this region, we are the saviours of Waziristan – what did you people have before we came? Nothing! You lived like animals, afraid of everything but God. Shut up and get in the van before I kill you and your *kafir drever*.'

He pushes her again with the weapon, knocking her on her shoulders for the second time. Mina catches the gun, catches it and pushes it back into the Talib.

'*Beghairat!*' she screams. 'You attacked that hospital – do you even remember its name?'

Both her sandals have fallen off her feet.

'You attacked the Hasan Faraz Government Hospital. That's what it's called. You attacked that hospital – for what? The newspapers told us you hit it because it took its name and its money from the state, from Pakistan, and from the army. You sent your men, your zombies, with RPGs to destroy it because you thought it treated those soldiers. But you bastards don't know anything – you don't know what Mir Ali is. We have been fighting those men since before you grew beards, before you learned how to read the Koran backwards. You didn't think about the victims of those killers who were treated in that hospital, did you?'

The Talib are hushed. They glance at one another nervously. The one who fell opens his mouth to protest the slight against their indoctrination, if only to reassert himself after such an inglorious injury has been done to him, but he clears his throat only to have Mina pivot and scream at him.

'Shut up!' She cries as she yells. 'I don't want to hear your sound.'

He steps back and holds his words.

Sikandar lifts his legs, like dead weights underneath him, and gets out of the van. He disturbs nobody and walks towards Mina. She is no longer surrounded by the Talib. They have all edged away from her. The commander signals to his men to back off. But Mina is stalking them now. She is circling the Talib.

The militants hit the operating theatre with the rockets as another man in a car stood watch at the entrance. After the explosion, the survivors in the hospital started to run away from the broken building.

'Did you watch them run for their lives?' Mina's feet slip in the mud as the words leave her mouth.

When those who could walk, who still had legs, began to escape, the Talib blocking the hospital gate exited the car and detonated the explosives packed in the trunk. Mina knows these facts; she knows the choreography of the attack front to back. She read survivors' accounts in the newspapers. She cut out articles from the Urdu, Pashto and English press. Mina searched obsessively for stories about the hospital attack. Months later she was still foraging for information, for light. Mina ripped apart newspaper after newspaper. She spent hours on the sports pages reading aloud every word. She even scoured the horoscopes for clues.

'At the sign of the first man –' Mina feels she can barely breathe – 'at the sign of the first man fleeing for his life, you set it off.'

The commander straightens his back. He knows the attack. Mina sees his recognition, she sees it, and as Sikandar approaches her, putting his arms round her to lead her back to the van, she draws a lungful of air and lets it out in a painful cry.

'You know. You know. You know. I can see it in your eyes. You know.'

Sikandar tries to lead Mina away, but she won't move. The Talib softens his stance, letting the gun fall to his side.

'This is a war . . .'

He tries to finish the sentence, but his tongue stalls.

'This is a war . . .'

Mina has no more strength left in her. Her muscles slacken and her face is drawn and emptied of colour.

'It wasn't his war. Zalan didn't have a side in the war.'

Mina speaks to the Talib differently now. She doesn't shout or yell. She withdraws her fists against him, exhausted by the force it takes to be so angry. The rain falls quietly so as not to disturb her.

'He died in between. They found his body in the parking lot. He was still alive. The people who lived said he was still alive, still breathing. But no one came. The doctors were pulling people out of the rubble of the operating theatres. They were moving people into the parking lot before the car exploded. They had to move them back, scattering themselves across the burning hospital compound in search of space to tend to the bodies that had survived.'

Mina's body heaves with each word.

Sikandar had been searching for Zalan in whatever parts of the hospital still stood. He saw the wreckage of the parking lot from the windows as he ran from room to room, as he looked in smoke-filled stairwells and the crowded emergency areas that were filling up with people.

But he didn't believe Zalan, little frightened Zalan, would be out there, where the damage had been most brutally inflicted. Sikandar hoped against all hope that he had been inside the hospital. Doctors pulled him into triage areas and tasked him with orders to start treating the wounded but Sikandar wrestled free, at one point stripping off his coat so people would stop grabbing his white sleeves for help. He tore through the grounds until he found himself at the hospital entrance.

He stood before the long driveway and counted the bodies before him. Two, six, eleven, fifteen. Eighteen, twenty, twenty-three.

He could no longer hear the cries around him.

Twenty-four, twenty-nine, thirty.

At thirty-three he saw the Bubblegummers.

At thirty-three Sikandar saw the trainers and moved towards the flashing lights as they flew between red and blue. And then he saw only one of them. Zalan had been moaning for help, the survivors said, but by the time Sikandar reached him he formed only the faintest breath.

Sikandar was on the ground of the parking lot, holding his boy's head against his body, pulling him, trying not to hurt him, but pulling him up. Zalan was so small. His limbs hung off his tiny body like strings. Sikandar could not look at him. He could not see what had happened to his son. He concentrated all his strength on lifting him, but he did not realize that he had fallen, too. Sikandar struggled helplessly until one of the nurses saw them and came sprinting over to help. The nurse called over another woman, a doctor, who lifted Zalan up, freeing him from his father's arms, and ran into the hospital with him. Dr Saffiyeh, one of the nurses told Sikandar, was very capable. She was their most committed paediatric surgeon and she would do everything she could to save Zalan's life.

But this was a war.

Everything she could do just wasn't enough.

'I came to claim the body,' Mina says to no one. 'I claimed what was left of him.'

Sikandar opens the door and helps Mina into her seat. He closes it and walks round the back of the van, away from the Talib, and once in his seat he turns the key in the ignition.

The commander raises his Kalashnikov and fires in the air as the Hasan Faraz Government Hospital van drives past the Talib and further into the forest.

24

The Chief Minister will soon be landing at the military base by helicopter. No one trusts the roads into Mir Ali, so the chief guest has been advised not to come by car. One can't ensure his safety overhead by airline either – the Miram Shah airport was the scene of a heavy siege only three weeks earlier. Gunmen encircled the small airport and fired at the parked planes, targeting the light-blue-and-white-camouflaged commandos stationed by the hangars. They were the most likely reason for the attack: people had spoken of repairs on military hardware being done on site by these pastel-wearing engineer commandos. It was two and a half days before the renegade gunmen were overpowered.

'Let us call a spade a shovel,' the Chief Minister intoned at the press conference he convened to discuss the dastardly terrorist attack. 'We are fighting forces who are intent on attacking the very people who toil blood and perspiration to protect their rights and their democratic freedoms. We are not going to give in to terrorists. They are envious of our values.'

Once the Chief Minister has landed at the base, he will exit his helicopter and pose for a photograph for the awaiting press. It is understood that he will then direct himself towards the assembled four hundred recruits, shaking hands and pinning medals on a few pre-selected, photogenic breastbones before taking to the podium to give his long-awaited commencement address to the would-be rebels who were being welcomed into the national army.

At the conclusion of the ceremony the Chief Minister has scheduled a session with the press, when he will answer questions and issue a final statement. Nasir will be there, holding a camera, replacing a cameraman who never made it from the capital. All the press today has been parachuted in – no local media outlets passed security clearance – but Nasir is a last-minute necessity. He has a Peshawar identity card and will be cleared by the major channel whose presenter is unable to simultaneously operate the machinery and narrate the day's proceedings. The anchorman has to be seen by his viewers, adequate face time is imperative. So too, then, is a replacement cameraman.

He must have already received the clearance. Nasir must already be standing in the press line awaiting the helicopter's landing.

Hayat keeps his hands curled round the motorbike's handles. His right hand is on the accelerator, pushing the rubber into his palm. Samarra holds his waist as tightly as before. She often rode with her hands burrowed in Hayat's pockets for warmth, holding onto him at the same time. But today she keeps her hands outside Hayat's jacket, though she allows her cheek to rest on his shoulder.

He is tired.

Hayat is so tired. He braces himself against the wind, shutting his eyes at traffic lights so that he can imagine that this day and all the others that will follow have already passed and left no perceptible trace upon him.

He wants to be done. It has been a long time coming, this feeling. Though it only recently reached fever pitch. Hayat grew up without a future. It had been denied to him; no one spoke of what he would become and what path would light itself in anticipation of his journey. Hayat had been raised only in the past – he had only memory, no right to imagination. Hayat spent his childhood at his father's knees as Inayat spoke to him of past wrongs, past injustices, past errors. There was no future, not for Hayat, not for anybody in Mir Ali, until those long agos could be righted.

And they could only be righted by the sacrifice of everything to come.

Hayat is tired of sacrificing and living among the ghosts of history. He had come of age under their sad shadows, and until now, until recently, until Aman Erum returned with nothing but a future attached to him, Hayat had not realized the volume of the sacrifice he had made so blindly.

Aman Erum swept barrier after barrier aside. He bypassed the deaths that had befallen their family, seeing only prospects for the opening of new doors and new ventures. No space in Mir Ali was forbidden for his growth. Aman Erum welcomed mourners with sombre handshakes and business cards – he did not break for funerals. He did not break for anything. Not for births, not for deaths. Hayat understood that the future was about movement. Ideas, trade, goods – the world and everything in it was in flux, travelling and shifting. It was the opposite of Hayat's condition. He was stunted by an unmovable injustice. It had grounded him and prevented him from seeing the wide latitude of opportunities ahead.

Hayat occupied the space his father had. The space his grandfather before him had, even Ghazan Afridi's unmade space. Hayat buried himself alongside them. In all these years he had never left their side.

Hayat had given his life to Mir Ali before he even had a choice. He thought of Zalan and lowered his head so that he would not cry. Not now, not here. Zalan had not given his life. It had been taken from him. There had been too much pain, too much death. Hayat counted his life in the days and months it had taken to reach this point. He had let too much time pass. He would end all that today.

It would be bigger than anything else.

Hayat did not feel prepared; he had not felt ready in the weeks and months of preparation for this. He could no longer sleep, he had not dreamed for days. Hayat shut his eyes against the wind. He had no choice but to go ahead with the day's plan.

Samarra shifts behind him. She moves her bracelet along her arm, tucking it under her sleeve as if it too requires warmth. She can't focus, though she tries, on the timeline in her head.

The winter calm of Mir Ali's roads, normally crowded with pedestrians and small vehicles, provides few distractions. There are no fruit vendors selling apples cooled in ice water. It's too early for the man who roasts corn over a sandy pit, plucking the kernels out with his fingernails and tossing them into the *lokhay*, squeezing lime juice and red chilli powder over the kernels, though the tastes in this mountainous area do not favour too much spice. There are few women on the roads this late morning; they are all at home preparing for Eid – dressing the children, plaiting their hair and painting their fingertips and palms with henna while the older women cook the day's meals.

Samarra thinks of her mother, almost certainly bent over the stove now, stirring too much black pepper into her lamb *saalon*. Samarra smiles. She lifts her face from Hayat's back and wishes he would look at her. It's too hard to speak to him over the roar of the motorbike. She wants his assurance.

Samarra thinks back to her phone and its dwindling battery. She wonders if Nasir has managed to record the statement he has prepared, using the same camera that will bring him into the Chief Minister's press conference. If they've searched him, looking too far into the pouches and pockets of his impressively sized camera bag, he's already dead.

By now the Chief Minister is making his chief guest's welcome address.

Security in Mir Ali is murderous, but all manner of rules are relaxed for the press. With ninety-plus channels on television and each station vying for dominance over listless national audiences, the press find few doors closed to their cameras and microphones.

Nasir should have got through after a perfunctory search. He will have been patted down and told to place his wallet and keys in a plastic basket while a bored police official pokes the outside of his camera bag before waving him through.

Samarra's phone has just enough battery left. She'll make the call in about twenty minutes. She tucks her bracelet deeper into her sleeve. The iron braid breaks a jasmine bud and cuts her skin. They are close. They have never been so prepared, so ready before.

But something is wrong. Samarra can feel it in her bones.

Noon

25

Hayat parks the motorbike by the mosque, its gate open wide as men begin to filter in, holding hands as they do in these parts, and wishing each other the coming of a happy Eid.

He lowers his foot to the ground and kicks the stand down to steady the motorbike. As the engine runs, his keys still in the ignition, the exhaust coughs out smoke that smells like burning rubber. He rests his hands on the handles.

'I'm sorry.' He says it to himself.

'Forgive me.' He whispers it to his father. 'None of us can be free.'

Hayat lifts his head and turns to look across the road. He sees him. Hayat nods his head in confirmation. I have her. She's here.

Samarra sits on the back seat of the motorbike with one foot perched on the bike's metal wing and the other placed for balance on the ground. She takes out her phone.

'I'll call in ten minutes,' she says. 'He's messaged. He's in. He's just waiting for the confirmation. They will have got the warning. They will have printed out the fax by now. They'll panic for five minutes, then compose themselves and wonder if this is serious. After another five they'll laugh at themselves for being so easily unnerved. And by the time anyone with any authority realizes that the threat came from us, that it should be sent upwards, it will be too late.'

Hayat is silent. He keeps his head bowed.

Samarra misunderstands the gesture. She assumes Hayat is

listening to her. She thinks he's keeping their cover and taking in her words.

'They won't have even seen it coming,' she says.

Hayat lifts his leg over the bike and stands on the pavement, broken concrete barely a step above the rocky, pitted road. There are palms here, too. Palm trees grow tall in Mir Ali. Hayat looks at the landscape around him. Including the mosque, it is uniformly grey. One-storey houses, unpainted, their cement dried and disregarded. Small businesses, *hotal* servers waving metal plates over large vats of hot food, roads that have been paved and then unpaved by machines and men.

The palms give dates, small wizened ones. They are not very sweet, but hard and tough to chew. In the summers they cut the fruit, still hanging off their yellow branches, and make a paste from them. But now, in the winter, the palms are bare and the skinny trees look Arabian and out of place.

Hayat understands there is little time.

'Samarra.'

He speaks to her now but she sees that he still can't look at her.

'I'm going round the corner for a minute. Don't move. Stay where you are, keep your head down. The crowds will thicken in a moment as the men begin to arrive for –'

She interrupts him. 'Where are you going?'

'They won't sound the *azan* till half past.'

He just wants to finish speaking.

'They come early, to hide their slippers and take seats at the back so they can chat when the mullah begins his sermon. Samarra?'

'Yes, Hayat *jan.*'

She is the only person, after his father, who calls him that.

He thinks of the insatiable king who lives alone on the

226

mountaintop because all the diamonds he desired had already been gathered and cleared. He thinks of the story his father always cut off before it reached the end, leaving the fakir stranded atop a cliff, suspended indefinitely. And for a moment Hayat wishes he was the fakir.

Looking around to make sure they are still alone, Hayat leans forward and takes Samarra's face in his hands. He kisses her on her eyelids, lingering on the one that encases the beauty mark in her eye.

'Hayat *jan*?'

Samarra looks around, to see if anyone has seen him place his lips on her, but when she looks back Hayat has already begun to cross the road. She watches him pause lightly on his heels, allowing the traffic to pass, before slipping into an alleyway that lies hidden under the low clouds of a rainy Mir Ali morning.

26

'Hello?'

'*Salam, grana*. What can I do for you? It is an honour for me to hear from you two times this Eid.'

Aman Erum holds the phone to his ear as he looks out onto the road.

'Have you received a fax, Colonel?'

The Colonel doesn't answer. Aman Erum hears him breathe into the receiver. It is a heavy, laboured sound.

'It's been sent by a woman I think you know. You may have met her once. Not so long ago.'

Aman Erum hears the rustling of papers. He turns his back away from the road. He doesn't want to look at her.

'I have her. She's here.'

'Is this a joke, *grana*? You are giving her to me?'

'She holds the key,' Aman Erum says slowly. 'Not me. I'm done. This is the last for me.'

The Colonel pushes back his chair. It sounds like a scraping, an unseating. The sound of more voices filling the room. The smart crack of ox-blood-heeled boots, the quick slam of doors being shut. A printer is sputtering out paper, maybe even a photograph. Someone is radioing a car. Aman Erum hears the Colonel clicking the phone onto speaker.

'No such thing, *grana*.'

'Did the fax mention who the target is?'

The Colonel falls silent again.

27

Sikandar drives quietly round the fallen waste of the forest, tree trunks cut down and splintered so that they open like artichokes, and clearings made of scorched earth and neglect.

The damage to the van is minimal, he sees that now as he glances around, noting that the original dents and scratches have been joined by only a few new nicks and marks. Sikandar's window is broken – this is the most obvious damage. Small shards of glass shimmer across the front seat. His legs shake as he examines the windows, nervously tickling the van's pedals.

His *shalwar* is sodden. The drizzle of the city falls harder out here as one circles the forest. The roads grow narrower and the air clearer. He is wet from the rain and from fear. But he is alive. They survived.

There is the smell of pine, late into the winter. It fills the air, the mountains, the woods. It has come to be a trademark of this fair tribal city, home for many years to thousands of men and saints, divine sometimes, princely at others. But it is not a kingdom; it is not a bastion of any empire. It has never been. Even centuries ago, when Buddhist avatars and princes walked the muddy tracks of the forest here, even then it was the home of ordinary men.

Fishermen sat on the banks of shallow streams with their *shalwars* rolled to the knees as they pulled in their catch. It was the home of those men.

It was the home of wayfarers and woodsmen, those that simultaneously worshipped the roots of their protective giants and then gutted them for sale. The wood merchants made key chains, they made plaques, clocks with steel numbers wedged into the pillowy beige bark. Some thought their trade tacky in later years, and of course it was. But they were only simple woodsmen then.

Times change and the forest thins. The pine scent grows familiar enough to be ignored, and the men, they come and go, leaving home for larger cities, for better trade. What more can they accomplish in their small home?

They would not have seen what was coming, not at all.

Sikandar looks at Mina and sees her eyelashes flutter, as if she is dreaming. Her lips murmur her secret prayers, incantations to keep her, at varying points, either brave or calm. She has been both, Sikandar thinks. And as he drives along the winding roads of Mir Ali's forest paths, the light rain falling on his windscreen, he hears the tap tap tap of tamarind seeds.

Acknowledgements

My thanks are owed to:

Carl Bromley for midwifing, for being such a friend.

Suhail Sethi for Pashto and our travels around the North.

Sabeen Jatoi for long ago.

Ghinwa Bhutto forever for her love.

Zulfikar Ali Bhutto for being the most supportive of all.

Mir Ali Bhutto, my Mir Ali, for being our brother and best friend.

David Godwin for saying one day: 'You should write . . .'

Sophie Hackford, Allegra Donn and Ortensia Visconti for their friendship. They have my fidelity, always.

Adrian Gill for encouraging and insisting, hongee.

Amanda Urban and Karolina Sutton for their faith and for taking so many chances.

Mary Mount for her enthusiasm, patience and extraordinary eye.

My dear Higgs for all her help and mms solidarity always when I needed it most.

Baba, for this book. It is yours. As is the title and my heart. In numberless forms, life after life, age after age.